TRAIL TROUBLE

TRAIL TROUBLE

WILL ERMINE

M. EVANS
Lanham • Boulder • New York • Toronto • Plymouth, UK

Published by M. Evans
An imprint of Rowman & Littlefield
4501 Forbes Boulevard, Suite 200, Lanham, Maryland 20706
www.rowman.com

10 Thornbury Road, Plymouth PL6 7PP, United Kingdom

Distributed by National Book Network

First paperback edition 2014

British Library Cataloguing in Publication Information Available

Library of Congress Cataloging-in-Publication Data

The hardback edition of this book was previously cataloged by the Library of Congress as follows:

Ermine, Will, 1888–1979.
Trail trouble, by Will Ermine [pseud.]
p. cm.
PZ3.D7845 Tl PS3507.R1745
38003524

ISBN: 978-1-59077-430-4 (pbk. : alk. paper)
ISBN: 978-1-59077-431-1 (electronic)

∞™ The paper used in this publication meets the minimum requirements of American National Standard for Information Sciences—Permanence of Paper for Printed Library Materials, ANSI/NISO Z39.48-1992.

Printed in the United States of America

CONTENTS

TRAIL TROUBLE

I: *"Stop Those Robberies!"*

THE Wagonspoke court-room, hot and stuffy this morning, was packed with perspiring men as the trial of five prisoners charged with rustling dragged on. It was an orderly, grim-faced crowd, composed of cowboys, freighters and ranchers. Some of these men were local. Others had ridden fifty, seventy, and even a hundred miles over the back trails to be here today, for word had spread far and wide that at last a shut and closed case had been drawn up against the rustlers who had harried the range for months.

The three men responsible for this difficult feat sat together at one side; ex-punchers, with the look of the saddle still upon them. The testimony of two of them showed an extensive familiarity with the law. The third, a big, red-headed man, displayed native shrewdness and an inarticulate dependence on action which lent humor to his laborious words.

Their cowboy days behind them, they had won their spurs as Pinkerton detectives. Their prowess had brought them to the Sweetwater Basin of Southern Wyoming to break up organized rustling; and they had done just that.

Bill Robuck slid his lithe, controlled body into the witness-chair again and again, patiently tying the knots of the net being woven about the accused. He it was who kept the district attorney, a pompous old bore, impressed with his own importance, pinned down to essentials.

"When you learned that the defendants were driving rustled stock out of the Basin," the latter propounded dogmatically, "and started after them, were you confident you could stop these desperate men?"

"The sheriff was forty miles south at the time," said Robuck. "Somebody had to stop them. We did it."

"Why didn't you call for volunteers?"

"I told you that the deputy sheriff denied his authority to act. With the defendants friendly with half the men in the county, we didn't have time to argue the matter. That's what we're doing now."

It went on like that while the court stirred restlessly and the prisoners glowered. Counsel for the defense did little better. His case was lost and he knew it.

"That's all . . . Call the next witness."

"Jack Deane!"

The muscular swell of Deane's chest and arms drew all eyes as he moved forward. His glance over the room from the stand was fully assured. He had an erect head and swarthy cheeks, and his bushy black brows made an unbroken line across the suavity of his face.

"Deane, when you and Robuck and Lefler closed in on the rustlers in Shoshone Canyon, did they fire first?"

"About once," said Deane dryly.

"Are you willing to swear these are the men who fired on you then?"

Deane's glance swept the prisoners and he nodded. "They're the ones."

"When three of them escaped, after the fight, did you go with Robuck when he went to round up these men?"

"No. I took after one of them alone. Robuck brought in the other two."

"Is Bill Robuck your superior?" the D. A. queried.

Deane hesitated. "Yes," he said then, without inflection.

Robuck was on his feet. "No, no. We work together." And to Deane: "You don't have to answer that question!"

"Never mind."

The prosecutor let his witness go. The defending attorney had little use for him. A moment later Red Lefler rose at a beckoning finger and tip-toed to the stand, a painful flush crawling up his raw-boned face.

"Lefler, when you were working alone, you saw these men—" the district attorney shot a dramatic finger at the prisoners—"blot the brands on B 4 steers?"

"Sure, I did. I had to—"

"You had to help them?" shot out the counsel for the defense.

Protest, muttering indignation, like a high wind through the room, and the gavel. The jury stared at Red Lefler expectantly, as quiet was restored.

"I had a hell of a lot of trouble to keep from helpin' 'em!" Red exploded. He was hot and flustered. Under cover of the open laugh which greeted his words, he muttered something that sounded like "Dang red tape!"

The judge banged his gavel smartly. "Silence in the court-room!" he roared.

He was old, stout and white-haired, and he was in his shirtsleeves; but there was plenty of dignity in his official frown. The room hushed.

"One more outburst like that," the judge barked, "and I'll—"

He got no further. With a savage flurry, at a guarded signal from one of them, the five prisoners galvanized into concerted action. The suddenness of it froze the court-room with surprise.

A slashing upper-cut dropped the jailer groaning on the floor, his gun clattering. A thrown chair caught the sheriff offguard. Staggering, he fell over a table, carrying it with him in a sliding crash which added to the confusion. The judge reared to his feet, bellowing with outrage. In an instant the room was thrown into an uproar.

Making a mad rush for the rear door, the rustlers lunged fiercely through the handful of men who barred their way. Their leader, a gaunt, swarthy man, smashed the door open with a single kick. A slug crashed into the wood a few inches from his head as he dashed through.

Letting out an uncontrollable yell, Red Lefler left the stand in a long dive. His big red hands closed on the collars of two luckless rustlers in the rear. All three came down in a heap with a shock which shook the building.

Jack Deane it was whose shot had so nearly cut down the escaping rustler. His six-shooter drummed again, winging one of the others, flinging him against a companion. In the split-second during which they fought to regain balance and plunge to their freedom, determined hands nailed them to the wall.

For his part, Robuck had been jostled and hampered at the decisive moment. He was not done. Wheeling, he hurled himself toward the open window. Three cowboys, perched on its sill, went over backwards with him as he plunged through. The group of hangers-on out there, craning their necks to see in, broke their fall.

Robuck found his feet somehow, savagely intent. Tossing men right and left, he made for the rear of the building, determination in the set of his lean jaw.

Behind the court-house a sharp clatter of hoofs arose. Reaching the spot, he was filled with chagrin by what he saw. The escaping rustler had picked a rangy roan belonging to the deputy sheriff; swinging up, he yanked the carbine in the boot. Its backward roar made Robuck throw himself to one side, answering with lightning swiftness, but without apparent effect. Men dashed out with ready guns, just as the rustler flitted through an alley onto the next street at a dead run.

Robuck sprang toward a near by pony. The sheriff grabbed him before he hit the leather.

"Hold it!" that official bit out swiftly. "That's the best hoss in town, he's got! Yo're needed at the trial. Lemme take care of this!"

Robuck saw reason without argument. Without delay, the sheriff and three men pounded away on the trail of the fugitive. Robuck pushed his way back into the court-room.

"Lafe Rash made good his escape," he reported.

"That bein' the case," the judge responded, glancing at his watch, "this court stands adjourned till after dinner."

The excited crowd poured out of the place, discussing the escape.

"Piece of dang foolishness!" Red Lefler pronounced it, with disgust, as the three sat in a hash-house eating. "Here I been ready for a good bust for three days. My tongue's plumb hangin' out, after the month we put in! But I s'pose after the trial's over, we got to head after Rash again." He shot a questioning look at Robuck.

"We'll have our bust," Jack Deane predicted easily. "Lafe will be over the line in Colorado before another day. Our job ends here."

"That the way you see it, Bill?" Red queried anxiously.

"It gravels me to see Lafe Rash make a clean getaway," Robuck answered slowly. "But unless we get further orders—"

"Whoops!" Red exploded, pleasure relaxing his features. "We'll have ourselves a time after all, huh?"

The thought plainly cheered the red-headed one, as the trial of the remaining four rustlers resumed that afternoon. Jack Deane was more brisk too, savoring the evening to come.

Robuck, no spoil sport himself, nevertheless felt his enthusiasm dampened as time passed and neither the sheriff nor Lafe Rash put in an appearance. The court knew what it meant. Rash was far away now, and still traveling. By way of making up for it, the jury made short work of the four prisoners. Each drew from eight to twelve years at hard labor, and the trial broke up.

"Wowie!" Red breathed a sigh of relief, as they left the court-room for the last time. "Now for a whirl at the bright lights and the laughin' water!"

"You goin' to wire the home office that we're done here?" Deane asked Robuck.

"Naw—don't do it!" Red urged, with comical earnestness. "Forget about it. Tomorrer's another day!"

Robuck smiled. "There couldn't possibly be an answer before tomorrow," he pointed out.

Nevertheless, Red hung back as they approached the telegrapher's office at the railroad station.

"Wire just come in for you, Robuck," the clerk announced, when they stepped in. "I sent it up to the court-house. Al musta missed you."

"You've got a copy, haven't you?"

The clerk dug it out. Robuck's brows drew down as he ran his eye over it.

"I don't wanta hear it!" Red declared, scowling in the door.

"You will anyway, I'm afraid." Robuck's smile was thin. " 'Report to Byrne, Captain of Detectives, Wells-Fargo main office, in Butte, Montana, immediately. T. J. Ferris, Supt.'," he read.

"That's a fine note!" Red wailed. "I knew this was goin' to happen! . . . Can't we put it off till mornin'?"

"That's not immediately."

"Well—it will be, then!"

Robuck, reluctant as he actually felt, was unimpressed. He made out his report. "What time is the next train north?" he asked the clerk.

"Six thirty-five."

Turning to his friends, Robuck's grin was rueful. "That's that. We've just about time to get our hulls from the hotel and grab a bite. It's ride all night for us."

"Aw, Bill—!" Red began. Even Jack Deane looked meditative.

"Nosir!" Robuck cut off their unofficial recommendations, firmly. "We'll take our fun where we find it, like we always have. In the meantime, the job comes first." Nor would he listen to further protests of any sort.

Byrne, the Captain of Detectives for the Western Division of Wells-Fargo at Butte, leaned back severely in his office chair, late the following afternoon, to survey the men before him.

"Make no mistake," he rapped out. "This is the toughest assignment you've ever come up against! Main-line trains have been held up three times in the last month between Twospot and Gray Bull, and gold shipments lifted. There's every reason to believe it's the work of one gang, with activities centering around Flathead. But they know my men. We're tied to a post.

I'm working now on the theory that strangers can get results where known men cannot . . . None of you have ever been in that country, have you?"

Robuck, Deane and Red Lefler murmured negatives.

"Your orders are simple," Byrne continued, as they talked the matter over. "I won't tell you how to go about your work—but stop those robberies!"

"And Mr. Byrne means at once," put in Ferris, dryly. That Pinkerton official had come on from Denver, to sit in at this conference.

Byrne nodded, his chin jerking downward with crisp authority. "There's no time-limit on your activities," he elaborated, speaking directly to Robuck. "If Smoke Devlin's wild bunch is behind this business, as you think, we want them captured, of course, no matter how long it takes." He paused. "Do you men know much about Devlin?"

Robuck assented for them all. "We know Smoke and several of his boys. I don't believe they know us . . . I've made a business of keeping track of Devlin's movements, in a general way, the last year or two."

"Good. And consequently you're sure that he's been active in that part of the state?"

"Yes."

Making a point of keeping in touch with drifting friends, Robuck thus came into possession of information of great value in his business. He had never tried conclusions with Smoke Devlin, but from the change in his demeanor since the mention of the outlaw's name, it was plain that he desired to.

"One thing more," said Byrne crisply. He eyed the three levelly. "Don't make any mistake about the caliber of the men you are up against. They'll call out the best you've got, and make you wish for more." He let that sink in. "I'll send our own man, Watson, to Flathead at once. They know him, and they'll watch him. That will give you a free hand. . . . Now, about getting to Flathead: Don't go there by the main-line, and don't go together. You'll have to use all the tricks you've got in the bag. There's a branch-line running up across the desert from Rocky Point that'll do."

After a few more words, the conference broke up. Drifting to the street, the trio stole looks at one another. All were conscious of what they were stacked up against.

"Nice job we picked," Deane commented satirically. "Smoke Devlin, in person!"

"Sure." Red brushed the fact aside, grinning. He had gotten over his disgruntlement of the evening before and was brusquely business-like. "This is just my size. How," he queried, turning to Robuck, "are we goin' about this?"

Robuck, revealing no more of his own keen interest than he usually did, fell to outlining their plan of action.

II: *On the Blackfoot Desert*

JOLTING, grimy, antiquated, the branch-line train from Rocky Point bowled north toward Flathead under an intense Montana sun. Robuck occupied a seat in one of its two cars, his saddle at his feet. He was alone; Jack Deane sat farther ahead, looking like a puncher on the drift. They had taken no notice of each other since boarding this tin-pot train.

Beyond the car window flowed the broken land on the edge of the desert; rocky, ridged, with an occasional high butte or barren mountain rising out of the hazy horizon. New country! Robuck unconsciously answered to the sight in an eager way. It was one of the secrets of his job—always to go on to new scenes, new people. His need for this was deep.

The passengers in the car shared his attention at intervals. He took his moment to think about each of them, until he came to the girl. Forgetting about general inventories at this point, he made a more intense and personal survey.

She sat a few seats ahead of him, on the other side of the aisle, so that he caught occasional glimpses of her interesting profile. Good-looking, quick in her movements, she wore a large sobriety. Her neat, small hat, her quiet traveling costume, revealed nothing of her origins; but her class was unquestionable.

"Soft brown hair," Robuck mused. "And I'll bet she's got brown or hazel eyes to go with it." Suddenly he wanted urgently to know.

The forward throw of his attention at length got to her. She turned, looked back—a direct, untroubled glance that touched him with awareness, and was gone.

"They're brown," he nodded to himself, with satisfaction; although it would have been the same had they been hazel. The view of her full face, soft with curves, yet somehow strong, had been even more gratifying than he had expected.

Jack Deane had noticed her too, he saw. Seated ahead, with his back to her, Deane remained that way as long as he could; then, his head turning, he let his eyes rest on her lingeringly.

"What's got into him?" Robuck thought, with swift irritation. "Don't he know any better than to stare at her like that?" The fact that Jack was something of a ladies' man, less likely to be considered rude than the average man, gave Robuck no assurance.

There were moments, however, when he forgot all about Deane, thinking of this girl. Who was she? He hoped she was going on to the end of the line; that she lived in Flathead, or near there. Perhaps a merchant's daughter, or a rancher's. Something in her eyes had said that she was not married.

Robuck thought of little else but her, until his eyes fell on the man.

He entered the car, this man, at the last stop before the train began its lumbering run across the forty miles of desert—a dusty, almost deserted way-station.

A man of fifty, tall and lean, he stood arrogantly in the door and ran his glance coolly over everyone in the car, judging them, passing them up—until he saw the girl. His face lighted. Coming forward at once, he took the seat beside her, settling back in a possessive way.

Robuck decided he didn't like him particularly. The girl spoke, and the man turned toward her deferentially. Robuck couldn't hear what was said, but it was plain that little interest lay on the girl's side. Reserve got into her manner; she glanced past the window repeatedly, as the train started up—as though she would have preferred to be alone.

"He's got a gall," Robuck reflected. He fell to studying the other. A blue serge suit, large ears, and the air of a successful business man, he ticked the details off. Again and again, as if conscious of the size of his ears, the man put up a hand to feel one of them, caressing its edges. The size of those ears seemed to measure his romantic appeal for any girl.

Whisps of smoke blew past the windows as the train ran out across the desert, a drab, brush-cluttered waste without distinguishing features. It was still a four-hour run to Flathead. Robuck was thinking how pleasantly the time would pass were he seated beside that girl, when her companion stood up, and excusing himself, drew a cigar from his pocket as he started back toward the second car. His eyes flicked Robuck briefly, a hard, level glance, as he passed.

"Wonder who he is?" Robuck thought idly.

Ten minutes later the monotomy was abruptly broken. A dulled snap and clanking rolled back through the rumble of the decrepit locomotive. The train began to slacken speed, coming presently to a shuddering stop.

Sitting up, the passengers looked around. One or two opened windows. Cries from the train crew floated in. After a long wait, the conductor put in an appearance.

"Break-down," he announced, in answer to a query. "A drive-rod snapped on us . . . Well, you'll have to wait, or walk. What? Oh—two or three hours."

"More like five or six," a disgusted passenger grumbled.

There was nothing for it but to exercise patience. One after another, the car windows banged open. The warm breath of the desert flowed in, and with it an idle lassitude.

Men got down to smoke in the shade of the train and discuss beef prices. The girl sat alone. Robuck remained where he was also, his glance reaching toward her. This was the time to get acquainted, he told himself. He wracked his wits for a plausible excuse.

Jack Deane was busy with similar thoughts. More than once he started to turn around and look at the girl, then caught himself. Presently, coming to a decision, he stood up. Saddle-bags in hand, he started out of the car. Robuck was mystified until, a few moments later, he caught a glimpse of Jack, building a small fire opposite the girl's window. Then he knew.

Deane was a coffee-fiend. He drank it at all hours and as often as he could. So real was his necessity that he carried a bag of it in his saddle-pocket. It had often cheered a long ride or a forced camp. Coffee was in his mind now.

It was past midday. Everyone on the train must be feeling the pinch of hunger. Robuck regretted his inability to go out and share Jack's coffee, as he had done often.

Evidently the girl felt the same way. Her glance strayed to the fire and the kneeling figure again and again as the fragrant aroma of boiling coffee stole in at her window. Deane had been waiting for just this. Catching her eye on him, he smiled.

"Smells good, doesn't it?" he said quietly.

"Yes, it does."

Her voice, full and rounded with amusement, touched off something in Robuck. It aggravated him that Jack should succeed in that which he had not even attempted. He started out of his seat and left the car.

Finding a trainman with a full lunch-bucket was an easy matter; persuading him to part with it was something else. At length Robuck parted with five dollars and promised to bring the empty pail back.

He found the girl with a steaming cup of coffee in her hand. Jack Deane was already on easy terms with her. He had come in and was seated in the back-turned seat opposite.

Robuck sat down, opened the lunch-bucket with a clatter, glanced up once or twice, and finally said:

"Perhaps you'd like a sandwich to go with that coffee. May I offer you one?"

She eyed him gravely. "You may if you wish."

He sprang up. The twinkle of partially-concealed mischief in her eyes as she made her selection told him at once where he stood with her, but did not dampen his spirits.

"Let me introduce you to Mr. Deane," she said, as Robuck continued to stand in the aisle.

He and Jack nodded suspiciously. After a moment's hesitation, Robuck extended the lunch-bucket as if he expected the other to refuse. Jack looked over its contents and took two sandwiches.

"Thanks . . . Have some coffee." He nodded toward the simmering can on the fire outside, but clearly had no intention of going after it himself.

Robuck looked disgruntled, and he was. Putting the lunch-bucket aside, he went out to pour himself a drink. When he returned, Deane had finished his sandwiches and was glancing expectantly toward the bucket once more.

Robuck offered the girl a second sandwich. She refused, but he pressed it on her.

"Thank you. They are very good," she accepted. "Won't you sit down, Mr. —"

"Bill Robuck," he said, complying.

"That egg-and-ham combination is particularly good," Jack remarked engagingly.

Robuck scowled. "Don't believe I've got any more of 'em." He made a pretense of looking.

"Yes, you have," said Jack persuasively, his expression bland. "There's one there."

Robuck took it out and put his teeth into it. "It is good," he admitted, sipping his coffee.

It was Jack's turn to scowl. "Maybe Miss Barron would've liked that," he said shortly.

"No, no," she protested. "I've had plenty." But her demure glance was appreciative as Robuck shot a wicked look at Deane. Apparently unconscious of the lively rivalry between them, she talked easily while the bucket was emptied.

An hour later they still sat together. Robuck and Jack spoke little, except to the girl, doing their best to conceal the impatience each felt. Deane wanted a smoke. Robuck, in spite of himself, was anxious to get on to Flathead and take up his work. Neither would leave, little as they felt themselves to be gaining with this attractive girl in the presence of the other.

The man with the big ears reentered the car. He strode forward to stop abruptly in the aisle, his eyes on the girl's face.

"Ah, Miss Barron. I've neglected you, I see," he said sauvely, in a tone of carelessly masked insolence toward her companions. "Perhaps you'd—er—prefer to sit forward, where it's not so crowded."

Robuck got up stiffly, a flush mounting his cheeks. Only the girl's presence held him silent.

"No, Mr. Mickle," she replied steadily. "I am getting along splendidly, thank you."

Mickle hesitated, his craggy face severe. He bowed slightly, turning away, obviously displeased. Robuck sat down and gazed after him.

"He is a business associate of father's," said Virginia Barron, in explanation.

"Mickle?" Jack Deane's brief tone asked more than mere corroboration.

"Yes. Mr. Mickle is president of the Flathead bank."

"He looks more like a cowman," Robuck commented, turning this information over in his mind.

"He used to be. He still owns a ranch—several of them, in fact." Her words carried a shading of disapproval.

"That kind of a banker, eh?" Robuck knew without being told that the foreclosure of mortgages was Mickle's game. Perhaps it accounted for the man's presence today on this train, beyond this desert. He found himself thinking even less of the banker than before.

Calls outside, and the stir of men, announced the arrival of a hand-car. "They've come to repair the engine," said the girl, leaning out of the window to look.

At this, Deane reluctantly went outside to gather his belongings. Excusing himself, Robuck returned the empty lunch-bucket to its owner.

"How much longer must we wait?" asked Miss Barron, on his return.

"Three-quarters of an hour, I'm told."

Better than an hour later, the conductor's call of "All-l aboard!" ran along the train. Passengers piled on. The train started with a jerk, gathered speed.

Robuck and Jack Deane still sat with Virginia Barron. Both had fallen under the spell of her laughing glance; neither was aware of the passage of time. They were surprised to find it late afternoon when the train slid through the outskirts of Flathead and began to slow for the station.

"Thank you—I shall manage nicely," the girl said

later, taking leave of them on the platform. "Father is expecting me."

"I hope we will meet again," said Robuck earnestly, his request to see her where she was going refused.

"Do you?" She smiled, meeting his glance.

"You may look for me also, Miss Barron," said Deane quickly.

She laughed, starting away. They watched her go. Robuck was thinking that he had never met a girl like her, absolutely without affectation, yet strangely exciting. He watched her cross the station yard and enter a store. Then, shouldering his saddle, and carrying his war-bag, he stepped into the street and headed for the hotel, without a glance for Deane.

Flathead was clearly a cow-town grown up. But the railroads had not come so long ago but that there was an uncurried look about the men in the streets. The saloons looked plentiful. Wanting to look them over at once, Robuck held off. He sniffed the dust and looked keenly at the ponies which kicked it up, his restless spirit coming to life. There was work to do here.

Reaching the hotel, he took a room, where he deposited his belongings. Jack Deane would take a room here also, when he got around to it. They would establish an intelligence liaison in good time.

Rolling a smoke, he looked out of the second-story window, over the roofs. Red Lefler had arrived in Flathead a day earlier. Undoubtedly he would have something to report. But it would be impossible to get in touch with him before dark.

With several hours of waiting before him, Robuck

left the hotel and found a restaurant, where he supplied the deficiency occasioned by the day's misadventure. His thoughts were busy with all that he had heard in the Wells-Fargo office at Butte, while he ate. With evening just beginning to arch overhead, a yellow glow which yet concealed the stars, he moved out to look the town over and size up his ground.

III: *Flathead*

PLAIN STREET was a blaze of light when Robuck returned to the hotel at eleven o'clock. Flathead was in full blast, and would continue thus for several hours, but he had seen enough for one night. His pause on the hotel porch might well have been for the purpose of finishing the smoke he tossed away as he turned inside.

Not once during the evening had he caught a glimpse of Red Lefler. Nor, cruising the saloons like himself, had Jack Deane. Robuck knew this because Jack had, by means of a guarded signal, imparted the information. Whether it meant that Red had left town in the course of his investigations, or that the red-haired one had come to grief at the hands of Smoke Devlin's followers, there was no means of knowing.

Of the presence in town of the outlaw's friends, Robuck had assured himself. Roy Olds he had seen at the faro board in the Ox-Yoke. Buff Ogle had been drinking with an unknown crony in another bar. It looked bad, in view of what Byrne had said about a leak concerning Wells-Fargo's activities; for there was every chance that this leak might extend to their own movements as well.

Climbing the stairs, Robuck was thinking of these things. There was no point in getting spooky, however.

He'd give Red until tomorrow noon, he decided. Then if the big fellow did not show up, they would have to trace him down.

Reaching the door of his room, Robuck paused. The hall was in deep shadow. Only the subdued murmur from the office below, the jangle of pianos from the street, reached this far. Putting a hand out, he turned the knob of his door and started to open it.

Its very silence gave him pause before the door had moved three inches. No click, no squeak—Robuck hadn't remembered that about this door. Hard on the heels of it came the unmistakable awareness of a presence. Someone was in his room, in darkness and silence —waiting.

Frozen there, his breathing suspended, he considered with lightning rapidity. Red Lefler was among the missing. Jack Deane he had left among the bright-lights. Which reduced his visitor to the status of an enemy. A saloon thug, ready to roll him for a few dollars? Maybe. More likely, it was someone who knew who he was and why he was here. Someone with the intention of settling his hash, even as Red's had been settled.

He saw himself lying in some alley, with open, sightless eyes. The picture brought a shrug to his lithe shoulders. Silently he gave the door a slight thrust inward, at the same time stepping back. No sound came from the bedroom. Flattened against the wall a few feet apart, his gun drawn, Robuck waited.

A minute dragged by, another, while he strained his

eyes. Then the vague shape of a head was thrust past the door-jamb.

"Reach, brother!" he snapped.

The head jerked back. Before Robuck could act, a stifled guffaw sounded, and the slap of a knee.

Robuck slid through the door in a flash, pressing it to behind him. His tone was disgusted: "Pull that shade before you light the lamp . . . How in hell did you get in here?"

Red Lefler scraped a match on his thigh, its bursting flame showing his broad grin. The shade had been drawn.

"Shucks, I trailed you and Jack for an hour," he announced, turning up the lamp.

"Why didn't you show yourself?"

"No sense in doin' that. I'm here now, ain't I?" He was as pleased as a kid over his own cleverness.

Robuck grunted, sinking on the bed. "Acting mysterious, the way you do, is the best way there is to get spotted."

"Have I ever been spotted yet?" Red flared.

"You'll cover it up quick, whenever it happens," Robuck grinned. "All but the last time, and that'll be too late . . . What's the news?"

The red-headed one opened his mouth to speak, when there came the faint scratching of a finger-nail on the door panel.

"There's Jack."

Red opened the door on a crack, then swung it wide, and Deane walked in.

"Here we are, eh?" was his breezy greeting. "Snug as a bug in a rug. What's the low-down?"

"Red was just telling me," said Robuck. He did not glance up at the other.

"Tell poppa too," Jack invited.

Red complied with all that he had learned during the last thirty hours. Smoke Devlin's bunch, he declared, had an established headquarters somewhere near town. Various of their number drifted into and out of Flathead at will. Red had identified half-a-dozen of them.

"This shore is a tough town," he added. "Can't tell me them fellers ain't known—yet they get around about as they please."

"How does it feel to have a town named after yourself?" Jack jibed.

"Who, me?" Red was affronted. "You mean I'm a flat—"

"Never mind," Robuck brushed all this aside. "Red, do these fellows seem to have plenty of money?"

"If gamblin' without much luck means anything," Red nodded, "they've got enough. They're takin' a lot of punishment at the cards."

"That settles it," said Robuck. "They're in on these express-car robberies, all right. What about the sheriff?"

"Wade Shandler?" Red thought a moment. "Well, he's a stodgy cuss, Bill. Pretty strict, I reckon."

"But not smart, like you, huh?" grinned Jack.

Red threw his hat at him.

There was more about the sheriff. "Any hook-up between Shandler and Smoke's men, that you could see?" Robuck queried finally.

"Nary a sign of it. Guess you can forget that angle."

"Smoke's getting his information from somewhere," Robuck pointed out. "Byrne said the long-riders never yet stuck up a train without a gold shipment aboard. That speaks for itself."

"It is a queer thing," Red agreed, puzzled.

"Our cue is to find that leak by elimination," Robuck pursued; "and plug it. I've gone over the ground in my mind already."

"I noticed you were thinking about it in the train this afternoon," Jack grinned at him.

Robuck frowned and his eyes darkened. He paid no attention to the thrust.

They talked for an hour in low tones. Finally Robuck stood up, unbuckling his cartridge-belt.

"You two better drift," he said. "And keep apart. But stay where I can tip you the wink."

The others rose. Waving an exaggerated farewell, Jack slipped away to his own room. His whole manner revealed how little he was troubled by the task they faced. A few minutes later Red left, going by way of the back-stairs.

Robuck sank on the bed, thinking over the events of the day. In spite of himself, thought of Virginia Barron broke in on him repeatedly. Jack Deane, it was evident, didn't get how he felt about her. Robuck mulled this for a moment, a furrow creasing his brow; then, putting it from him, he prepared for bed.

A banging on the door awoke him in the morning.

Making a grab for his pants, he opened the door slightly. A boy pushed in, a grimy envelope in his hand.

"Robuck? . . . Yeah, a telegram. Sign right here, mister."

Robuck took the envelope, eyeing the messenger. "Who are you?" he grunted.

"Johnny Brumster. My Pop's baggage-man, down to the depot," the boy supplied, waiting hopefully.

"Brumster?" Robuck fumbled in his pocket. "I'll just buy that name from you. How much do you want?"

The brown hand jerked back suddenly. "No yuh don't!" He looked cheated and disgusted.

"Well—" Robuck tossed up the dime he had fished out. "You can have this anyway, if you feel that way about it."

The boy gone, he ripped open the wire. Reading, he whistled lowly, then grinned.

"Expect baby Wednesday night. Joe is eleven. Love." It was signed, "Bertha."

Robuck knew from this that a gold shipment was coming through. "Joe is eleven," said that it would be on the west-bound, sometime after eleven o'clock. "Bertha" stood for J. M. Byrne; and "love" meant, in plain terms, "get on the job!"

He looked up. Today was Wednesday. Tonight was the night, and there was still plenty to do.

Dressing hurriedly, he descended to the street, and, breakfast over, sauntered out. Jack Deane, he guessed, had not yet risen; but Red Lefler loafed in a saloon door, the day before him, and apparently nothing on his mind.

Their impersonal glances met as Robuck walked past. Only Red saw the crumpled ball of paper that dropped by Robuck's heel and rolled toward the step.

The big fellow remained where he was for a moment; then stepping down, he seated himself on the step, where he proceeded to roll a smoke. This done to his satisfaction, he pulled out a match, which slipped out of his fingers. Picking it up, at the same time he got the wadded ball. Some minutes later, in a deserted corner, he unrolled and read it.

"Gold coming through on tonight's express. Keep your eyes open and be in the room at dark," it read.

Reading it through twice, Red touched a match to its corner, and snapped his fingers hastily as he dropped the burning fragment.

"Tonight, eh?" There was no flutter of excitement in his literal soul. "That means we gotta be on the job!"

Passing down the street, Robuck headed for the main-line station. It was a wooden affair of considerable size. Circling around to the platform, he looked it over, and then, entering the waiting-room, asked for a time-table. With this in his pocket, he went out and settled himself on an empty baggage-truck.

The west-bound express was due in Flathead at eleven-forty-seven that night. The nearest previous stop was at Waukena, at eleven-five.

Past experience indicated that the outlaws would know about that train and what it carried. The problem was to discover at what point they were intending to strike. Could it be done?

Strolling up Plain Street half-an-hour later, he paused beside Jack Deane, standing on a corner. Jack's elaborate casualness said that he knew what was afoot. Robuck murmured low words, which reached just far enough.

"Find out if Devlin's crowd has faded. Keep an eye on 'em. If any leave, tip me off."

Jack made no reply, walking away.

Stepping into a saloon, Robuck ran his eye down the bar. None of Smoke Devlin's friends were present. Entering the Ox-Yoke a few minutes later, however, he found Buff Ogle taking a drink. It was unlikely that Devlin would operate without Ogle. Something of Robuck's tension relaxed.

He remained in the place for an hour, a glass at his elbow. Ogle showed no inclination to leave. When Red Lefler walked in, Robuck, giving him a look, sauntered out.

It was a long day, a trying day. Between the three of them, they managed to keep track of four members of Devlin's gang, none of whom offered to leave town until, late in the afternoon, Robuck watched Buff Ogle emerge from the telegraph office, stuffing an envelope in his pocket, and, mounting his horse, jog away to the south. Five minutes later, swinging up on a rented animal, Robuck hurriedly followed.

At first he thought he had lost his man. Then he found Ogle's tracks in the south-running road. Shortly afterward, pushing ahead briskly, he caught sight of the other. Ogle was taking his time. Hugging the scant cover afforded, Robuck kept him in view.

Half-an-hour's ride from Flathead, Ogle turned into a branch trail, and a little later, pulled up before a sprawling, log-constructed ranch house. The place stood on an open flat and there was no safe means of approach. Robuck contented himself with watching from afar. Ten minutes passed before Ogle reappeared, to jog back the way he had come.

Robuck beat him back to Flathead. He saw at once, as Ogle swung down before the Ox-Yoke, that the man carried news. Following him into the saloon, Robuck watched him walk up to a card table at which Roy Olds was holding forth.

No word passed between Ogle and the gambler. But Robuck caught the look exchanged across the table, and knew a signal had been passed. Then Ogle turned and went out.

"He's passing the word along," Robuck nodded to himself. His lips drew flat. "And I've got to find out what that word is, and where it came from."

Hopeful of intercepting a sign which might identify for him other members of the outlaw gang, in the meantime, he trailed his man. His purpose was defeated by the fact that Ogle had a speaking acquaintance with countless punchers. He spoke or nodded to almost everyone he met.

Turning Ogle over to Jack Deane with a sign, Robuck gave up and headed for the telegraph office. Except for the telegrapher, the place was empty. The man looked up inquiringly.

Flirting back his vest, Robuck flashed his Pinkerton badge, at the same time producing his identification card. The telegrapher read it.

"All right. What'll it be?" he said.

Robuck swore him to secrecy, and then said bluntly: "Buff Ogle came in here an hour ago and picked up a wire. I want to know what was in it."

"I don't know—" the man began.

"You will know!" Robuck caught him up quickly. "I'm investigating these express-robberies. This concerns them. Any hesitation on your part will lay you open to a charge of obstructing justice."

The telegrapher scowled, but he was convinced. He dug out of the records a copy of the telegram in question, and handed it over.

"Who's this Jim Barker it's addressed to?" Robuck asked.

"He owns a little spread, three-four miles out of town. Ogle carried it out to him."

Letting his eyes drop, Robuck scanned the scrawled words on the paper. Suddenly his cheeks went lean and red with anger. He stared. The wire was identical with the one he had received early that morning: "Expect baby Wednesday night. Joe is eleven. Love." But before the signature, "Bertha," had been added four words which he had not seen before: "Aunt Minnie notified also."

Robuck's eyes came up blazing. There was no doubt now that Jim Barker was a mask under which Smoke Devlin received information of impending bullion shipments. His scalp crawled as he realized that Devlin had been at the ranch to which he had trailed Ogle. Moreover, the outlaw had been doubly warned. Robuck's knuckles whitened as he held the telegram.

"Aunt Minnie is a new name for a detective," he thought, grimly.

IV: *Red Plays a Hunch*

ROBUCK'S first thought was that the outlaws knew about him and his companions. But, returning to the street while he considered the possible source of this leak, he presently found reason to alter his ideas.

He rejected at once the slim likelihood that anyone in the employ of the express company was passing out information. It narrowed down, in his mind, to someone in the telegraph office at Butte. Robuck saw at once that it would be impossible for that person to learn that Pinkerton men had been sent to Flathead. When the wire announcing the bullion shipment went through his hands, he could have known only that it was addressed to a detective, and would think, naturally, that it was another Wells-Fargo operative.

Watson, the express detective, was now in Flathead. Smoke Devlin's crowd would watch him, believing themselves otherwise in the clear. Robuck saw an unexpected advantage in the inevitable vagueness of code telegrams.

Turning back up Plain Street, he was snapped to attention by the sight of Roy Olds mounting a hammer-headed roan before the hotel. Olds swung the pony out and rode down the street. At the next corner he turned south, and Robuck knew that he was on his way to receive his orders, as Buff Ogle had done. It called for no undue apprehension; Robuck made no move to follow the man.

Ten minutes later Ike Geer, a bearded, saturnine man, followed Roy Olds' example, swinging into the saddle and drifting out of town. Presently Tom Baggs did the same.

Seeing this, Jack Deane looked across the street with his brows lifted queryingly. Robuck shook a faint negative. These gents would be back, his manner said. Ogle was their magnet—next to Smoke Devlin himself, he was their boss.

Red Lefler, lounging against a porch-post a few doors away, observed this exchange of signals and gathered their import.

Following Buff Ogle into a restaurant at suppertime, however, Robuck thought it odd that none of Devlin's crowd had come back yet. Glancing around the tables, his eye fell on Watson, the Wells-Fargo man, a few seats away. Watson, a heavy-faced man, appeared interested in nothing but his meal; but Robuck got the impression that he was keenly conscious of Ogle's presence, for not even by accident did the detective's glance stray toward the other.

When Ogle, finishing first, got up to leave the place, Robuck received an abrupt shock. Crowding past Watson's table, the outlaw looked the detective full in the face—and smiled.

There was so much malicious triumph in the expression written plainly upon Ogle's callous countenance that Robuck's throat suddenly dried. He half-rose from his chair. It came over him in a flash that by watching Ogle so narrowly, he had allowed himself to be tricked.

Leaving the restaurant hurriedly, he was bent on making sure. Nowhere did he find any of Smoke Devlin's men. They might have faded into thin air, so complete was their disappearance. Robuck, seething with exasperation, got a firm grip on himself, forcing his wits to a clear comprehension of his vital mistake.

Now that it was too late, it was easy to see what had happened. Buff Ogle had fully expected to be watched. He had acted as bait, to throw the watcher off the scent while the rest of Devlin's crowd slipped away unremarked. That Ogle thought Watson, the Wells-Fargo man, to be the one who trailed him, was immaterial. His ruse was no less successful. Even now the outlaws, with the exception of Ogle, were foregathering at some unknown point, preparing an uninterrupted reception for the bullion train.

Robuck made the rounds, a fury of action on him, but with hopeless anger burning in his heart. He was looking for his partners. Spotting Jack Deane at length, he threw caution aside and strode directly toward him.

"Gypped!" he ground out, lowly. "Ogle's the only one of the gang left in town—and I just saw him laugh in Watson's face! I suppose you know what that means."

Jack swiftly sobered. "So!" he murmured dryly. "I can guess." He gathered himself for what was to come.

"Where's Red?" Robuck shot out.

"Don't know."

"We've got to find him, and dammed quick!"

Separating, they made a search for the red-headed one. It was without avail. Red Lefler had disappeared as completely as the outlaws had done.

"Maybe he stole a march on us," Deane suggested, meeting Robuck in an alley.

Robuck didn't think so. "You know Red. He saw me tip you off to let Smoke's men go, when they headed for Barker's spread. He's probably somewhere taking it easy."

"You told him to be in your room at dark," Jack reminded.

"We can't wait that long!" Robuck was savagely impatient. He thought a moment, came to a decision. "Get down to the livery stable and grab yourself a horse," he directed. "I'll be waiting south of town."

Five minutes later they met on the road.

"Where we going?" Jack inquired.

Robuck told him about Barker's ranch, and what he had seen there. "There's no question," he added, explaining the second telegram, "that Smoke was at that ranch at the time. And that's where his bunch collected. Our one chance is to spot them there, or pick up their sign."

They rode rapidly as far as the branch trail leading to Barker's ranch. Swinging wide then, they approached the flat from cover and looked the cabin over.

It appeared deserted.

"Three, four," Jack murmured, counting the ponies in the corral.

"There were five, this afternoon," said Robuck

tersely. "That means that Smoke has left. with his men." His tone was grim.

"We going to ride in?"

"No point in that. We'll circle for sign. We haven't much time to spare."

Already the sky was yellowing with sunset. In a few more hours, the bullion express would be held up and robbed—and Robuck would not even know where, unless they found a plain trail leading away from this ranch which would give him the direction.

A mile or two from the house, they made a complete circle of Barker's ranch. The tracks of several cow-ponies were found, but these without exception were a day old, at least. While this did not mean that none of the stony trails had been used, it gave them no help.

The sky was thickening with dusk as they returned to the point from which the circle had started. Deane shook his head, his black eyes quizzical. "That settles that," he said practically. "Now what?"

Robuck was filled with chagrin. "Don't make any mistake about the caliber of the men you are up against," Byrne had told him. He had done just that.

"We can ride our heads off," he said slowly, "and get nowhere fast in this game. We'll go back to Flat-head. Buff Ogle," he proceeded, thinking out loud, "is one smooth hombre. I'm not entirely satisfied that a stick-up will come off with him thirty or forty miles away. It isn't in his book. We'll have another look at Ogle."

The lights were glowing by the time they reached town. The evening's gaity, undisturbed by premonitions, was getting under way. Buff Ogle sat in the Ox-Yoke, a glass at his elbow, cards in hand. He was quite at his leisure. Robuck turned away from the door, a spark of determined resentment in his eye.

"He's safe for an hour," he told Deane. "Come on up to my room. We'll think this thing over a little more."

Separating, they reached the hotel by different ways and met in the upper hall. A bar of light showed under Robuck's door. When they stepped in, there was Red Lefler reclining on the bed, his boots off and his hands behind his head. An expansive grin split his rawboned countenance.

"Where in hell have you been?" Robuck rapped out.

"I been around," Red answered, defensively. "Whatsa matter?"

"We've lost them, hide, hoof and horns, that's what!" Robuck sat down disgustedly.

Red, struggling up on an elbow, was comically startled. "Did Ogle do a fade?" he demanded unbelievingly.

Robuck spread his hands. "He's here. He's the only one who is." He explained how Ogle had practically laughed in the face of Watson, the Wells-Fargo detective, and why.

To his surprise, Red settled back, relieved. "If Brother Buff is still in town, that's all right, then. I reckoned I had him figgered."

"What's this?" Robuck demanded.

Red grinned. "Hunch. I told you I been around," he pointed out. "Instead of forgettin' about it, I followed Baggs out to that ranch, this afternoon; and I watched what happened. Them gents are here in town right now, waitin' in a shack. And Devlin's with 'em!"

Robuck and Deane exchanged a startled glance.

"But Ogle and Watson—" Jack began.

"That was jest a trick," Red scoffed. "They wanted to throw dust in Watson's eyes, and they done it."

"And in mine too!" Robuck chuckled. He could appreciate a joke at his own expense.

It put another face on things. They discussed the situation at length, ironing out their course of action. At last Robuck blew out the lamp and turned to the door. They stole down the back stairs. By means of alleys and cluttered back yards, Red led the way to a stable on the edge of town.

Here, on a blanket spread on the straw, with a masked lantern for light, half-a-dozen men played cards, murmuring in low tones. Robuck, through a crack in the weathered boards, identified Smoke Devlin and read the crude force of the man, a strange excitement working in his veins. The outlaw had twinkling, shrewd eyes in a lined face, and studying that face, Robuck realized that there was nothing small or petty about its owner. In another field than outlawry, Smoke Devlin might have been a liked and respected power.

Robuck drew off, his mind in a whirl. Even now it seemed incredible that the outlaws were here—that they meant to hold up the bullion train and rob the express-car in Flathead.

"Keep an eye on that stable," he told the others. "I'm going to keep tabs on Ogle. It's around ten o'clock now. If those men leave inside of an hour, let me know immediately."

After a few more words, he left. Ogle was still in the Ox-Yoke. He had finished his game and stood at the bar, talking to the same man with whom Robuck had seen him the previous day, on his first sight of the outlaw. Far from confident that he had identified all of Devlin's friends, Robuck looked this man over carefully.

He was forty-five at least, stout, blear-eyed, carelessly dressed. He had a cast in one eye. All about him were the signs of failure. Robuck decided he didn't like his looks. Catching the bartender's eye on him, he jerked his head toward Ogle's companion.

"Cattle buyer?" he queried carelessly.

"Used to be," was the response. "Mebby he is yet. I dunno what he does. . . . Broke Horan," he added, naming the man.

Robuck filed the information away.

For the better part of an hour Ogle and Horan argued amiably. Robuck would have found it difficult to believe that anything was on the mind of either, had he not known what he did.

At eleven, Red Lefler walked into the saloon, ordered a drink, tossed it down, and walked out. Robuck followed him. Once beyond the door, his indolence left him; he found Red waiting behind the building.

"What's up?"

"Ike Geer left the stable, ridin' his hoss and leadin' five others," said Red. "He got out of town, circled around, and come back across the tracks. The hosses are in that deserted ice-house a hundred yards from the station."

"Good," Robuck nodded. "I suppose Ike went back to join the bunch?"

"Didn't wait to see." Red hesitated, then said: "Bill, shall I lift them hosses? We'd make a clean round-up, if we put 'em afoot."

It was a tempting proposal, but Robuck demurred. "It would only tip them off," he pointed out. "The last thing they'll do before the train comes in will be to make sure of the horses."

"What about Watson?" Red persisted. "You goin' to put him wise?"

"I don't know why we should, and I know a swell reason why we shouldn't. They're watching every move he makes." Robuck mused a moment. "We know all we need to, now. It's forty minutes till train time. Go get Jack," he told Red, "and meet me behind the station restaurant."

Red faded into the shadows. Ten minutes later, he, Deane and Robuck met at the appointed place. They crossed the street, avoiding the light, and approached the station. A night-clerk worked at a telegraph key in the office. No one else was about.

"Devlin will soon get here," Robuck murmured. "We've got to know where he'll hole up, and then pick a likely place for ourselves."

They moved along the dark, beaten-earth platform. Suddenly Robuck snapped his fingers, pointing. "Of course! They'll crawl under the freight platform." He shied away from the spot, an ideal one for the outlaws' purpose, and they paused to consider their own best bet.

Red leaned idly against a large tool chest, the property of the maintenance department. Deane, pulling him away, looked the chest over thoughtfully.

"Just the thing," he murmured, "if—"

The chest was locked. Jack pried out a staple with his gunbarrel, lifted the lid. The chest had been practically emptied by some track gang working up the line. Moreover, it had slots in each end through which watchful eyes might probe the night.

"How about it?" Jack asked Robuck.

The latter nodded. "The engine ought to stop within fifty feet of us," he said.

In two minutes they were crouching in the box, the top lowered.

Time dragged interminably now. Watch carefully as he would, Robuck could detect no slightest movement in the vicinity of the freight platform. He was not deceived. It was almost a certainty that Smoke Devlin's gang was there, waiting.

"Train's late," Red whispered, stirring restlessly.

Robuck made no reply, straining to hear. At last he was rewarded. Faint at first, then swelling to a sustained roar, the rumble of an incoming train made the night tremble. A swath of faint light cut down the track, grew stronger. With a wind-whipped shriek of its whistle, the night express thundered near. It began to slow. The weight of its big drive wheels shook the tool-box, and the hiss of the air-brakes was loud.

No sooner had the big locomotive ground to a panting stop than Robuck, peering through his slot, made out a number of shadowy figures, running through the gloom. Something rose in him sharply. Gun in hand, he straightened, putting the pressure of his back against the box-lid.

"Now!" he cried.

V: *Smoke Devlin's Style*

ROBUCK was the first one out of the tool-box. Red and Jack were at his heels in an instant. They had barely gathered themselves when, above the panting breath of the engine and the hissing release of the brakes, they heard the sharp slap of running feet and hoarse cries.

The head of the train had pulled past them; they were opposite the first car. The open fire-box flung a red glow against the night. Even as he wheeled that way, Robuck caught a flash of two men on the ballast, starting to mount to the cab. He was dimly aware that Red and Deane sprang the other way, toward the express-car; then he forgot them.

Plunging forward, he flung a shot at the second outlaw, just as the other pulled himself into the locomotive cab. Surprised, the man wheeled around. In the brilliant orange light, his face was masked with a bandana, as was that of his companion. Robuck had no idea who they were.

The guns of both punctured the night with staccato savagery. Robuck flung himself aside, firing back. His was the advantage for the moment, in that he had their figures silhouetted; but he knew if they were not dislodged immediately, the iron bulwarks of the cab would make their position impregnable. Gathering himself, he charged straight into the mouths of those belching guns.

The engineer was crowded into a corner of the window-seat behind his throttle, his hands up. His face was pasty. The fireman, caught in the tender, was of different mettle. Robuck saw him throw himself forward, his face tied in a knot of rage, his shovel raised. One of the outlaws, getting a flash of him out of the corner of his eye, whirled sidewise, chopping at him with his gun-barrel. The blow caught the fireman alongside the skull. He stiffened, then crashed down, the shovel clattering.

Lead fluttered past Robuck's head with a wicked back-draw as he neared the tall step. A slug carried his hat away; another, striking his empty holster, jerked him around just as the crouching outlaw above loosed a lethal blast in his face.

His answering shot took his antagonist in the arm. The man reeled, caught himself. With a wrathy snarl, the second outlaw, kicking the fireman aside, brought his guns to bear and cut loose.

Robuck's bullets clanged and rattled off the metalwork of the cab. The wounded outlaw, emptying his gun, flung it in a sudden fury.

"By God, I'll finish you!" he yelled. He hurled himself straight at the man on the ground, his wild whoop echoing.

Caught by surprise, Robuck snapped two lightning shots into his chest, and dodged. He was not quick enough. The man, dead in the air, struck him a glancing blow, slamming him aside, and thudded dully on the ballast.

Robuck regained his balance, blind determination in the set of his jaw, and charged the steps. The remaining outlaw, getting a flash of that remorseless face, threw a panicky shot and stumbled over a lump of coal as he backed away. When he recovered, Robuck was nearly on him. A slug took him in the elbow. His gun clattered. With a bellow, he abruptly gave up, whirling toward the other side of the cab platform and sailing down the steps into the darkness in one reckless leap.

The racketing pound of six-guns could be heard from down the train. Robuck knew the fight was concentrated at the express-car. He wasted no time.

"Douse that fireman—get him on his feet!" he hurled at the bewildered engineer. "Then pull out of here in a hurry!"

Grabbing up a drinking bottle, the other stuttered something; but Robuck had not waited for a reply, leaping to the ground over the body of the dead outlaw and starting down the train.

Orange flashes stabbed the darkness back there with unbelievable rapidity. Yells rang out, harsh and unbridled. Robuck slowed as he neared the express-car, questing the night for Red and Jack.

Plainly the car-door had not been forced as yet. There had not been time. Muffled thuds sounded from within as the express guards fired through the car sides; and although two minutes had scarcely elapsed since the train had ground to a halt, already the raking fire of Lefler and Deane had taken effect on the outlaws, routing them. The licking muzzle-lights of their guns showed at the car-ends and under the car, where they had taken refuge in the heat of the attack.

"Red! Jack!" Robuck cried.

"Here!" Red's bull-like bellow came to him out of the darkness.

"Smoke 'em out of there!" Robuck flung the sharp command. He had thumbed his gun full of fresh cartridges as he ran forward; it spat into the shadows under the car. At that moment, with a snapping, grinding jerk, the train started.

Robuck was aghast.

"My God, they'll be cut to mince-meat!" he burst out. The grim significance of this fight was swept out of his mind in a flash. "Crawl out of there!" he roared.

The firing broke off abruptly. Without a thought of his own safety, Robuck sprang to the side of the moving car. Red and Deane were with him, ready to yonk back to safety any sprawled outlaw whose limbs were endangered by the merciless wheels of the car-trucks.

Not one madly struggling figure could they find. At the first warning tug of the locomotive, the outlaws at the car-ends had scrambled over the couplings to the far side of the train. Those crouched underneath the car had flung themselves toward the far side.

"Around the end of the train!" Robuck called sharply to his partners. "Maybe we can nail them!"

Squealing, groaning, swaying, the train gathered speed. It was already going too fast to allow them to swing through between the cars. They charged toward the twinkling light on the rear car. As it flitted past, they wheeled across the empty tracks, heading for the abandoned ice-house, looming blackly against the night sky.

The muffled pound of pony-hoofs sounded beneath the diminishing roar of the train, as the trio thrashed close to the ice-house through the brush. A low call rifled across the darkness; a six-gun flashed, raking the brush with lancing fire. Robuck answered those shots; but doing so, he knew they were too late. A dark group of ponies drew swiftly around the corner of the ramshackle building and thundered away into the night.

Robuck lowered his gun. Red was close beside him.

"Dang 'em!" the latter ejaculated. "They sure are slippery gents!" He turned. "Good chance of catchin' up with 'em, Bill. I reckon I marked a couple."

"We might do something by daylight," Robuck responded. "I winged one, myself, who'll lose some blood."

The thunder of guns at the station had been heard on Plain Street. As Robuck and his companions returned to the dark platform once more, a crowd began to pour along the side of the station.

"What's goin' on here?" demanded an authoritative voice. Wade Shandler fronted the trio, his eyes snapping in the soft light from the station office.

"Smoke Devlin's wild bunch tried to stick up the express," Robuck told him. In a few words he explained what had taken place. "Somebody better step in the office. I imagine the clerk has been hog-tied," he wound up.

"How come the train pulled away so quick?" Shandler demanded, as several of the crowd moved into the station. "It stopped, didn't it?"

"Two men took charge of the engine crew," Robuck told him. "I jumped them, drove them off, and told the engineer to pull out pronto. One of that pair," he added, "is down the track a couple of hundred feet. I think I finished him."

A railroad man, attracted by the excitement, approached bearing a hastily lit lantern.

"Bring that here," the sheriff directed. The crowd started down the platform. They found the dead man where Robuck had said he would be.

"Sho! It's Tom Baggs," a man muttered in an awed voice, as the outlaw was turned over.

Baggs had been shot through the arm, and twice through the chest, one of the bullets having evidently pierced the heart.

"Wal, that's good work," Shandler admitted grudgingly. His eyes returned to Robuck. "Who are you—Wells-Fargo men?"

"No," a rasping voice put in. Watson, the express detective, stepped forward, his expression gloomily. "They ain't. I'll vouch for that."

Robuck flashed his Pinkerton badge. Deane and Leffler followed suit. A change came over the crowd, hitherto somewhat reserved, if not openly suspicious.

"Oh," Shandler grunted. "Pinkertons, eh?"

"By God," a man burst out; "they done a good job! That's the first bullion car that ever got by Smoke Devlin's guns!"

Others broke into admiring murmurs. Once the story

was complete, the discussion began. Red Leffler found himself answering eager questions bearing on the feelings of a man who, with only two companions, dared to tackle Smoke Devlin's uncurried mavericks. Even Jack Deane unbent, his swarthy face impassive, but pleased. Robuck alone bothered to remind himself, in the midst of this adulation, that their work was only partially done.

Baggs, the luckless outlaw, was carried away. Robuck and Shandler, the latter putting routine questions, started up Plain Street with Watson, the Wells-Fargo man, at their side. The crowd followed. Rapidly, the news of the attempted hold-up and its foiling spread over Flathead.

At the sheriff's office, ten minutes later, Robuck finished his talk with Shandler and turned away to make his arrangements for horses the first thing in the morning, when daylight might give them a chance to pick up the outlaws' trail. At the door, Watson stood staring into the night, a displeased expression in his eyes.

"Watson, this was just a bad break for you—" Robuck accosted him.

The man snorted. "Break, hell! I wasn't even notified that a bullion shipment was comin' through!"

"No. It wasn't safe. Devlin's crowd knows all your men; I found the leak that's been putting you on the shelf. It'll be worth your while to do something about it." Robuck explained about the two telegrams. "It's pretty plain that someone in the telegraph office at Butte is tipping off the outlaws," he concluded. "If you move carefully, you ought to be able to close in on the guilty man."

Watson was both amazed and grateful. "I sure will see to that, Robuck!" he declared. "And thanks! You're givin' us a chance to save our faces!"

Robuck brushed this aside. He could not deny to himself, however, that his successful campaign against the long-riders up to the present, gave him deep satisfaction. It was the kind of work for which he was known over thousands of miles of range.

He was turning away, when a man on foot burst up the street in a state of exhaustion, yelling weakly and waving his arms excitedly. Robuck, sensing trouble instantly, started forward. Red Lefler, who was beginning to grow impatient with the crowd of admirers who wouldn't leave him alone, broke through them roughly, reaching the running man before Robuck.

Grasping the man, he supported him, listening keenly as hurried words rattled out. Stiffening at what he heard, Red let out a wrathy bellow.

"God A'mighty!" his roar smote the arrested listeners. "Smoke Devlin got the damn train, after all! He rode out and nailed it at the water-tank, a mile west of town!"

Consternation sank its barb into Robuck's heart. Here was something no man could have foreseen. The incredible truth stared him starkly in the face. Devlin had robbed the train in spite of everything!

Wade Shandler had heard. Bawling a harsh order for horses, he ran forward. He and Robuck extracted what meager information was available from the man who had run the mile from the scene of the hold-up with the news. Five minutes later Shandler, Robuck and his partners, and a dozen other men, swung aboard ready horses and pounded west through the outskirts of town.

A disused trail ran out to the water-tank, along the tracks. The posse covered the distance at a gallop. The train was still there, just getting ready to pull out, its lights burning through the night. Shandler had the conductor hold it up, while they had their look, and shot flashing questions.

Smoke Devlin's crowd had made short work of the express-car this time. Its door, wrenched off its hinges, hung sagging. Inside, a wounded guard lay groaning on the floor. Another sat propped against the wall, blood soaking through his shirt. The safe had been blown open and stood gaping emptily.

Devlin's gang, the bullion in their possession, had ridden away to the north.

Without delay, the posse swung away from the train, heading into the night. An hour's steady riding took them into broken hills. They pressed on.

Robuck, dazed by the rapidity of this night's events, had nothing to say. Recovering, he was aware of a dull, sustaining glow of anger against the outlaw who at the outset had nearly outwitted him, and then finally had succeeded in doing so. He should have been warned by that glimpse of Smoke Devlin's shrewdly humorous features through the boards of the stable in Flathead. He *had* been warned. And then this had happened.

Red and Deane were busy with similar thoughts, as the night wore on. All their sense of triumph was gone.

They had nothing to offer as dawn broke, revealing no slightest trace of the outlaws.

"Mebby they doubled back south," Shandler's deputy, a grizzled little man with a twisted foot, suggested.

Another man laughed mirthlessly. "Mebby they flew," was his retort. "It's all one to us, looks like."

The posse turned back, pursuing its investigations. There was nothing to be found. Midmorning saw the cavalcade riding wearily into Flathead, empty-handed.

"What'll you do now?" Lefler queried gruffly of Robuck, as they reached the street after taking care of their ponies.

"Go to the hotel and pound my ear," Robuck answered shortly.

There was little else to be done. Even Jack Deane, usually so resilient in the face of adversity, was content to turn toward the hotel without comment.

Flathead was filled with people today. Men had arrived from all over that country, attracted by the night's occurrences. Many were the quizzical stares, glinting with scarcely-concealed amusement, which followed as Robuck and Deane entered the hotel and mounted to their rooms.

Robuck was so chagrined that he had no thought of food. His tenacious mind was questing forward toward the next move in this grim game. Pulling his boots off, he flung himself on the bed. Despite his restless thinking, fatigue bludgeoned him; in ten minutes he was asleep.

He awoke late in the afternoon, the low sun flashing

across his face from the window. Sitting up, he swept the room with a glance. On the floor lay a scrap of paper evidently thrust under the door while he slept. Rising, he moved forward to pick it up.

> Sorry old man but I needed the money (the penciled words ran). Youre game but slow My hats off to you if thatll help.
>
> Smoke Devlin

Robuck sank on the bed, studying the scrawl, a pucker between his brows. It was at once a defy and a challenge to some queer, twisted sort of sportsmanship which existed in the outlaws leader's game and rugged frame.

"So that's the kind of a terrapin he is," issued from Robuck's flat lips.

VI: *Mickle Issues Orders*

RED lounged in the office of the hotel, waiting, when Robuck came down. Despite his attitude of ease, there was a worried expression in his puckered blue eyes. He got up with guilty haste, as though he were somehow to blame for the misfortune which had overtaken them all.

"Wire here for you, Robuck," the clerk announced. "It came half-an-hour ago. I thought you wouldn't want to be bothered," he added apologetically.

Robuck said nothing, taking the telegram and tearing it open. He stood for some time, studying it. Not once did Red's solicitous gaze leave his face.

Jack Deane came down the stairs at that moment. He had recovered his affability, at least in seeming. "What's up?" he inquired imperturbably, seeing the paper in Robuck's hands.

" 'Report back to Butte at once,' " Robuck quoted dryly, turning to him.

Red's face fell. But Deane only said: "From Ferris?" in a tone of mild curiosity.

"Yeah."

"He knows," Jack nodded.

The three moved out to the porch and took chairs. In late afternoon Flathead was not busy, but there were men about who noted the presence of the discomfited Pinkerton detectives. Compressed smiles were visible. The trio paid no attention, absorbed in the decision which rested with them at this moment.

"Yes, Ferris knows—and Byrne knows," Robuck said matter-of-factly. "There's only one meaning to this order." He sounded thoughtful.

"Takin' us off the job," supplied Red lugubriously, his blunt face more than usually homely as it reflected his thoughts.

"Not if I know it!" Robuck retorted sharply. "This thing is beginning to get personal with me."

They looked at him. Without more words he produced the note from Smoke Devlin which he had found in his room. Jack read it and handed it to Red. The latter's cheeks took on the brickish hue of his hair. He growled in his throat.

"Why, dang his ornery hide!—" he began.

"You see how it is," said Robuck softly.

They nodded briefly. "I don't like leavin' unfinished business, myself," Deane commented. "We never did it before."

"And we won't this time. It'll mean our jobs; but no brushloper can put over on me what Devlin did, and get away with it." Robuck spoke with suppressed force. His raking glance was keen. "I mean to do something about it. Are you with me?"

Deane murmured, "I expect," composedly, and Red said earnestly: "Whatever you say goes, Bill. You know that."

"You don't have to do this," Robuck warned them.

"It may be a long grind, and I'm ready to take Devlin's trail alone, if it comes to that."

"The hell you will!" Red thrust in indignantly. "Whadda I care for Pinkerton's, in a pinch? They'll git you killed and dock you for neglectin' to report the matter; there never was a time I didn't know that. If they think we're no good, that's too bad. We can still skin our own skunks, I reckon!"

Robuck nodded, repressing a thin smile.

"The motion is made and carried, that we smash Smoke Devlin," Jack summed up laconically. "I wonder," he added, addressing Red amiably, "whether you could be persuaded to stay overnight in the same state with Devlin, if it weren't for Bill Robuck."

"What's that matter?" demanded the literal Red, in an incensed tone. "I'm stayin', ain't I?" The truth was, there were no grounds for Deane's jibe; Red's nerve was unquestioned and notorious; but he needed only the flick of his friend's tongue to set him off.

"Then I'll wire the home office," put in Robuck, who was used to these baitings, "to hunt for three good men to replace us, effective immediately. Is that right?"

Deane stood up with him. "That's right. I'll go along with you and take a real look at this town." It was his pretense that most of his not-inconsiderable work he did without more than half trying.

On their way to the telegraph office they ran into Virginia Barron. It was the first either had seen of her since the train. Emerging from a store, her arms piled with packages, she was plainly a rancher's daughter, the regular contours of her face framed in a broad-brimmed Stetson. Trim, soft-leather boots encased her feet. About her lips played a quick smile of recognition.

"Miss Barron," Jack saluted her suavely, lifting his hat. "Allow us—" And he began handing her hundles to Robuck.

She laughed frankly. "I should scold you for the deception you practiced on me at our first meeting," she told them. "I was appalled at the rudeness of each of you to a stranger; and it was only familiarity!"

"I'm afraid there was a measure of necessity behind that trick," said Deane easily.

She changed swiftly. "Of course I know there was." She was gazing at Robuck now. "I'm sorry about the abominable luck you had with Smoke Devlin," she told him, her glance commiserating. "No one could have seen that coming."

Jack chuckled. "That's what Bill has been telling himself," he put in shrewdly.

It was true, and Robuck took no exception to it. He was thinking that Jack's ready tongue put him at a disadvantage, but he only said: "Devlin will find that this doesn't end the matter."

She nodded understandingly, and, he thought, with approval. "He has had his own way too long. I've heard Mr. Shandler say so often."

There was a touch of feather-light malice in her tone as she spoke of the sheriff. Studying her face, Robuck thought better of whatever he had been about to say.

"I told Father I'd meet him at the bank," she continued, as they turned to go on. They headed that way, talking easily. Virginia's head barely reached to Robuck's shoulder, as she moved between him and Jack; yet he could not escape the feeling that somewhere in her small body she packed as stout a spirit as either of them. Something about her appealed to him even more strongly than before. Deane felt the same way, if his manner meant anything.

Reaching the bank, Robuck thought it odd that her father should have business there at this late hour; for she paused at its very door.

"I'll take my packages now. And thank you," she smiled.

Robuck handed them over. They were saying good-by, when the shade-drawn door of the bank rattled and swung open. Virginia's father and Duncan Mickle emerged.

Dale Barron was a red-faced, ruggedly built man of fifty. There was a solidness about him, a staunchness which Robuck immediately liked. Just now he wore an air of heavy preoccupation, which lifted as he turned.

"Here you are, Ginie," he said, smiling down at his daughter.

"Father, I want you to meet Mr. Robuck and Mr. Deane," she said. Her introductions included Dunc Mickle. The banker's acknowledgments were dry, but Barron was almost cordial, his deep-set eyes twinkling.

"I heard about you two before I knew what you were," he said, in his deep rumble. "Somethin' about a train, if I remember right . . . This country can use a few more like you."

"Well, Barron," Mickle put in, with smooth formality; "I'll see you later, then." He tipped his hat to Virginia and turned away.

"I take it you're stayin' on, after what's happened?" Dale Barron continued, to Robuck and Jack.

The former nodded. "We'll be around a while," he responded tersely.

"We're spendin' the night at the hotel," the rancher remarked. "It must be near supper-time."

They turned that way, Barron falling in beside Robuck, and Jack with Virginia. Dusk sifted down over this town's roofs; the heated air was cooling.

"The Flathead range needs cleanin' up," the girl's father declared; "no doubt about it. These train hold-ups between here and Twospot are only a part of what's goin' on. My stock is bein' rustled steady; I've been gouged bad. Other owners from here to the desert are in the same fix."

"What is your brand?"

"Cross 8. About ten miles south." Barron invited Robuck and his partners to ride out and visit him. "I expect your outfit's plannin' to make a clean sweep in this country, or bust somethin' tryin'?" he pursued.

"Pinkerton's? . . . No." Robuck was short. "We're quitting them today."

Barron sobered, scanning his face sidewise. But, warned by something in Robuck's tone, he did not press his inquiries.

At the hotel the group broke up. Robuck had yet to get his telegram off to the detective agency. He and Deane turned back. Five minutes later they were wording the message which conveyed their resignations.

The wire dispatched, they returned to the street with the definite feeling that they had burned their bridges behind them.

Returning to the hotel, they passed the bank once more. Jack was on the inside. A tall man, his eyes just came up to the level of the large shade across the bank window, running up from the bottom. A light burned within. Deane saw Dunc Mickle seated at a desk in the rear of the place. Opposite him sat a lanky, drab man with a closed face, at least sixty years old.

Deane did not realize the importance of that conference, passing on, and he neglected to mention what he had seen. "There's one banker who keeps long hours," he reflected idly.

Mickle did. Twenty-four hours a day were not too many for the kind of business he was in. Long years of chicanery and sharp dealing had whittled his face into lean severity. His expression, however, was seldom more revealing than at this moment, as he stared across the desk at Spokey Withers, his carved cheek-bones prominent, his thin lips tight and ruthless.

"I'm particularly opposed to these railroad jobs," he was saying. "Every time Devlin makes a haul, he's just that much harder to handle. If he gets nailed one of these times, we'll lose him altogether."

"You can't say that kind of thing to Smoke," Spokey pointed out, a timeless patience in his bent shoulders and his faded old eyes. "He knows how you feel—but what you want of him is only a part of his activities. We got to remember that."

"I know it." Mickle scowled, his head bent forward.

"There might be something in making that bullion hard to dispose of," he continued suggestively, a crafty light in his eye.

Spokey shook his head decidedly. "It'd only drive him out of the country, Dunc," he said. He thought a minute. "No—there ain't much you can do with Smoke Devlin. He values the protection you give him jest so much; beyond that he won't stir a stump . . . What's on your mind?" he went on, in the same mild tone. "Ain't Barron about ready to give up the ghost anyway?"

Mickle's glance sharpened. His voice took on a grating tone. "He surprised me," he said, frowning. "He was in here and paid up that mortgage not half-an-hour ago. I didn't think he could do it."

Spokey watched him without change of expression. Despite his appearance of indifference, all his faculties were bent on the problem they considered. Ten years ago Dunc Mickle had saved him from a heavy prison sentence and given him a job. Since that time, the law had not existed for Spokey, save as Mickle chose to manipulate it. Loyalty to his benefactor had become a habit which he found no occasion to break.

"Smoke's boys have been eatin' into the Cross 8 reg'lar," he said musingly. "Barron must've stripped his range to raise that money. He's hangin' on by his teeth, Dunc."

"But he's hanging on!" Mickle snapped impatiently. "I should think Devlin would consider it a pretty soft thing to be covered on the bunches he drives through the hills, and be allowed to keep every cent he gets for the stuff at the same time. He don't act that way. Why, he should've had Barron on his knees and hamstrung, by this time!"

"I've let him know you think so," said Spokey quietly. "But, Dunc, he's got his side of it too. You can't threaten him and make it stick. He says if he works too fast, the Stock Association'll find a way to jump him in spite of you."

"Poppycock!" Mickle scoffed dogmatically. "I promised him he wouldn't be touched, didn't I? He's just finding excuses. If he doesn't get busy in short order, I'll find some means of seeing to it that he does!"

He was almost savage, thinking over his imagined injuries at the hands of this outlaw on whom he had so little leverage. His indignation was not lessened by the fact that in spite of his harsh words, he would have thought long and carefully before turning his single weapon of betrayal against Smoke Devlin.

"Spokey, I want you to give it to him straight from the shoulder," he directed. "Ride out there right away. I expect him to go after Barron, and finish the job. That's little enough to ask for what he's getting. Tell him that!"

"I'll tell him," said Spokey. "If he's back yet."

His employer appeared about to explode in exasperation. "He'd better be back!" he snapped. "If he ain't, wait for him. Don't leave him room to make any mistake about it: I want that ranch, and I mean to get it!"

Spokey nodded, unmoved by the other's vehemence. "But don't expect Devlin to jump jest because you crack the whip," he warned. "He'll be more apt to come through if you put somethin' in his way that'll make it worth his while."

"Good God!" Mickle whipped out furiously. "He's got a free hand, hasn't he?" But he saw sense in Spokey's words, and cooled rapidly. "You don't think the steers he's drivin' are enough to satisfy him?" he demanded keenly.

Spokey's smile was slow. "I don't know. But if a little sweetenin' would make things move faster—"

A pulse beat in Dunc's bony forehead. "Offer him a thousand dollars on those terms," he grated. "If it takes a little lead to discourage Barron, all right. I don't care what he does. You and he ought to be able to think of something. I don't want to know what it is, do you understand? I don't care; what I want is results!" A purple tinge came into his parchment face and his hand trembled. "Give Devlin to understand that if the Cross 8 isn't in my name before long, it's likely to go hard with him, and that's final!"

Scraping his chair back, Spokey got up. "All right, Dunc." After a few more words, he left by the back way. There was something ominous in his mildness as he moved off through the darkness without hurry, his head bent thoughtfully. He appeared merely a harmless old man, musing on the past.

VII: *A Man's Job*

ROBUCK'S thoughts were never very far away from his work. Accordingly, it was not without design that he, Jack and Red sauntered down Plain Street that evening with their eyes open.

Reaching the Ox-Yoke, they stepped in. They found a place at the lower end of the bar, away from the sizeable gathering at the roulette table. Downing his drink, Robuck hooked an elbow over the rail, and, attracted by a grumbling monologue from that direction, let his eye run over the poker tables.

Something snapped to alertness in him as his glance encountered Horan, the broken-down cattle buyer whom he had seen with Buff Ogle, sitting in.

Horan was the author of the dogged and half-angry discourse. With him at the table were a bearded freighter, a town sport, and a young fellow, little more than a boy, in the garb of a cowpuncher. It was toward the latter that he directed his taunting, heckling remarks, and the reason for this was plain. Before the boy stood an ever-growing stack of chips; while that before Horan was as steadily diminishing.

"Can't tell me my luck is as bad as this," Horan flung out discontentedly, shooting an ugly look across the table.

An angry flush crept up the boy's temples and receded. He had plenty of nerve, but he was having trouble with his temper. Studying the lean, beardless face, Robuck found a likeness which he could not place.

A hand ended. The boy raked in another pot. Horan flung down his cards with a curse.

"What in hell you got up yore sleeve?" he demanded offensively.

The boy stiffened. He had held his tongue as long as he was able. "What do you mean by that?" he snapped.

"You oughta know what I mean," Horan sneered. "Lay off the crooked stuff—if I gotta name it for you!"

It had been the boy's turn to deal. Flying into a rage at the bald words, he leaned forward and flung the deck into Horan's face.

"By God, nobody can tell me I cheat, and get away with it!" he spat out.

Broke emitted a wrathful snarl. Flinging his chair back, he jammed the table aside, lunged with the ferocity of a cougar. The boy's gun sprang into play, glinting in the light. Horan knocked it aside, fastened a merciless hand on the other's shoulder.

He was a hulking brute, twice the size of the boy. He could have man-handled him with ease; but before he had time to set himself, Robuck thrust roughly between him and his victim, forcing them apart. Horan was hurled violently back. A lean, hard face on the level of his own, met him with scornful condemnation.

"You can't make it stick, Horan!" Robuck told him thinly. "I saw the whole thing. The boy didn't cheat—but you'd like to!"

Broke glared, rage and hatred shaking his raw-boned

frame. Recognizing his assailant, he froze. Craft stole into his drink-sodden visage.

"The Pinkerton, eh?" he jerked out. Sarcasm edged the mocking words. "The range detective that never loses! Always on the spot—like you was last night!" And he laughed cuttingly. "Go back where you come from," he ground out, in a taut tone, "and send us some ten-year-old kid with brains—"

He got no further. Robuck's fist, flashing up, collided violently with the side of his head. Horan went backward with a crash that shook the building. He scrambled up with a roar.

The entire room was watching. A silence hung here, laced with tension. Scarcely a man present was unaware of Broke Horan's devious nature, and his potentialities.

"Hold on, here!" an authoritative voice broke in, before Horan could reach for his gun. Dale Barron strode forward, decision in his mien. "If there's any shootin' done, it'll go hard with you, Horan. Take your hand away from that gun!"

"I started this," Robuck cut in coldly. "Let him finish it, Barron, if he wants to!" He had nothing but contempt for Horan; but the taunt the man had flung in his teeth had lit a fire in him which he preferred to quench with violence.

"No," said Barron stolidly. "We'll put an end to this, here and now." He turned to the boy whom Horan had accused of crookedness. "Cash your chips, Sam, and clear out of here. I'd have thought any son of mine," he reprimanded, as the other complied, "would have sense enough to steer clear of a tinhorn like Horan. But mebby you've got to learn."

Sam Barron darted an angry look at Broke, moving out. Robuck had not once taken his eyes from the glowering cattle buyer. The man's treachery was fathomless. Robuck knew he had made a deathless enemy of Horan, but it had been inevitable. Cooling rapidly, he no longer wanted to rub out the man who held the answers to a number of questions which plagued his mind. But it suited his purpose to give no hint of this.

"Horan, you don't look satisfied. Maybe you'd like to step outside and settle this," he invited thinly.

Wade Shandler, hurrying up the street, stepped in at the moment. His keen glance took in the principals. He heard Robuck's challenge, and Horan's angry mutter, but did not wait to gather its import.

"Never mind, Robuck," he attempted to take charge. "I'll handle this. As I understand it, your work lies in another direction."

While there was nothing here to take offense at, his meaning was plain. The censure in his tone, born of a limited officiousness, stung Robuck to a hot retort.

"Whatever you understand, Shandler, get it in your head straight that I'll jump any cheap crook that gets in my way. I don't have to tell you this will be a better place to live in when a few of them have been run out. What you do about it is no concern of mine. But I intend to get some of them, and get them right. That goes for Smoke Devlin, and right on down the line to the small-fry!"

A cold-steel determination rang in the words. Not a few of the listeners found themselves beginning to respect Robuck in a new way. And among them was one who found no cause for rejoicing in that enforced respect.

Standing at the bar, Dunc Mickle had seen the whole affair. He took Robuck's measure now with a sharpening interest, a faint scowl darkening his aloof face. Hitherto he had seen this man as merely a meddlesome detective with an exaggerated opinion of his own powers; but now he read in him a cold force of resolution which it would be dangerous to ignore.

Robuck's declaration of intentions had climaxed the moment. Finding no adequate response to the merited rebuke, the sheriff merely shrugged. Broke Horan turned away in a murderous mood.

"Much obliged for standin' up for my boy, Robuck," said Dale Barron. What he had seen made him like the younger man more than ever. "Horan's a shady snake. Sam won't make the same mistake about him a second time," he chuckled.

Robuck turned the matter off easily. Barron was about to propose a drink when he caught Dunc Mickle's eye on him. The banker jerked his chin imperatively. After a word or two, Barron turned that way.

"We'll go up to the bank now, if you're ready," Mickle told him. While there was little the rancher could tell him that he did not know, it was a matter of common prudence to see that Barron and Robuck were kept apart.

Leaving the saloon, they walked up to the bank.

"Now, what's this you mentioned in connection with the Association, this afternoon?" Dunc opened up, as they faced each other across his desk.

"I said I want a special meetin' called. Somethin's got to be done, Mickle. This rustlin' is not only bad—it's gettin' worse. As head of the Stockman's Association, you can see my position . . . They been gettin' into you pretty deep, too, ain't they?" he broke off.

"Yes," Mickle nodded, his glance thoughtful. He had seen to it, with his usual perspicacity, that the three ranches under his control did not appear entirely to escape the stock losses which harassed the other spreads. "I've had an armed guard over my herds for some time. Even so, I seem to suffer along with the rest."

"That's jest it!" Barron smote the desk with his fist. "We got to get up on our hind legs and act. I tell you, what I learned while I was makin' the gather for this last beef cut, scared me. If it don't end mighty quick, I can't hang on."

"The Association's doin' all it can. You ain't the only one that's spoken to me." A bland look appeared on Mickle's face. "Far as you're concerned, Barron," he went on, "my offer for your ranch is still good. I may be makin' a mistake," he admitted, with an air of frankness; "but I'll stand behind my own figure, if you say the word—take the place off your hands."

Dale Barron shook his head. "I won't accept that price for the spread I've built up," he said, stubbornness getting into his voice. "I won't take any price. I don't want to leave, and I won't be driven out either!"

But he looked worried. "What's the latest report of this man Daggett we hired?" he changed the subject.

Mickle told him the investigator had turned up nothing as yet. They talked it over. Finally Barron said:

"There's a thing I've had on my mind since suppertime—these Pinkerton men. Robuck told me they was quittin' their jobs today. Mickle, they know this kind of work. Why not hire the three of 'em?"

At the first mention of the Pinkerton detectives, Mickle's glance sharpened. When Barron finished, he shook his head decidedly.

"No," he said. "I can't see it. The idea is all right," he softened his rejection cautiously; "but we know nothing about them."

"We know all we need to! They stopped Devlin cold, right here at the station," Barron pointed out warmly. "And you saw Robuck in action tonight. He's had rotten luck, I know; but there's no doubt in my mind that those gents have got plenty of guts."

But Dunc was unpersuaded. "After what happened last night, they're washed up in this country, and they know it," was his opinion.

Barron showed ire. "I'll speak to 'em for myself," he declared. "I can afford to pay their salaries, and more, if this rustlin'll only stop . . . You heard Robuck say they'd stay here and do a job on Devlin," he reminded forcefully. "Smoke knows plenty about the rustlin', all right!"

Mickle had not expected him to take this stand. He found himself forced into a change of front. The last thing he wanted was for Robuck and his partners to remain in the Flathead country. But if they were determined to remain anyway, and this appeared only too likely, his wily brain told him it was better to have them in a position where he could both follow and anticipate their movements.

"Well-l," he said, as if unwillingly impressed; "maybe there's something in your suggestion, after all. No use of you goin' to that expense, though. I'll get hold of Robuck tomorrow and sound him out."

"Not tomorrow!" Barron insisted. "Right now, if you're goin' to do it at all. Good God, man—this is serious!"

Cursing in his heart, but with outwardly calm demeanor, Mickle gave in.

"We'll get it over with, if that'll relieve you," he said, rising. "Probably they won't even talk job, after just quitting one. But we can try."

"Yes—and close with 'em, if it's possible," Barron added firmly. "If you can't square it with the Association, I will, myself!"

Red Lefler, his arms hooked over the bar, watched Broke Horan move away after his clash with Robuck. There was a faintly contemptuous glint in his eyes. He had not the same reasons for suspecting Horan that his partner had, but he thoroughly disliked the man.

"Shucks!" he grunted, when Robuck rejoined him and Deane. "There ain't no fight in a crowd of his kind. Reckon we'll have to stir up our own excitement." Hand in pocket, he moved toward the roulette wheel.

"Come back here!" Robuck told him sharply. "None

of that for you, bucko. We need every cent we've got. We'll have to buy ponies in the morning, and we've got to go on eating, too. Get out of your head the idea that you're having a lark—we're going to stick this thing out."

There was no fun in his voice, and Red did not argue. When Robuck and Jack swung out of the place a moment later, he followed—albeit not without a backward glance of longing. Red had neglected to take life seriously for so long that he had almost forgotten how.

Reaching the hotel, Jack would have taken a chair on the porch, but Robuck said shortly: "We'll go up to my room." Once there, they fell to a consideration of their position.

Red thought a job would be comparatively easy to acquire. Robuck proceeded to disillusion him.

"We don't want a job punching cows," he pointed out. "We must be free to go when and where we please. We can't afford to be tied down."

Jack nodded confirmation. "We'd better concentrate on putting Smoke Devlin out of circulation in a hurry," he said. "My guess is that we'll never find the kind of jobs we'd like. We might as well forget it."

They were still discussing it, pro and con, when a brisk knock sounded at the door. Robuck opened it to find Barron and Mickle standing there. The banker was inscrutable, but Barron appeared intent.

"Glad we found you," he began, stepping in. "There's a little matter I'd like to see settled right off." He met their suddenly arrested glances for a moment, and then came out flatly: "Look—what would you three say to a job?"

Robuck's appraising eye slid from his face to that of Mickle. "It depends on what kind of a job it is," he responded, not a little surprised at this turn of events, but still not particularly hopeful.

"I reckon you know we've formed a Stockmen's Association here," said Barron. "Mickle is the head of it. I told you about the rustlin' that's goin' on, this afternoon. I've persuaded Dunc that you're jest the kind of men we need. We'd like to have you sign on with us."

"Stock detectin'? Unh-uh." Jack Deane shook his head. "I'm afraid that isn't up our road."

"Done it before, haven't you?'

"Yeah. But, you see, right now—"

"Wait a minute." Barron was sure of himself. "Robuck said somethin' about goin' after Smoke Devlin. And you don't want to be steered off it . . . Well," he added triumphantly, "what would you say if I tell you Devlin is behind this rustlin'? Mickle don't think so, but I got reasons to believe I'm right."

"That would make ours and yours the same job," said Robuck slowly. "Tell us more about it."

They talked it over at length. Dunc Mickle found an irony in the fact that even he put in an occasional word to persuade these men to accept the task of running down the rustlers. Robuck finally nodded, glancing at his companions. "I'm for accepting the Association's offer," he proposed.

"Sure," said Red. Jack also signified his agreement.

At this point, Mickle had his say as to what their duties would be. Robuck cut him off. "We're always open to suggestion, and of course we'll act on all information—but we handle this our own way, or we don't take the job," he said abruptly.

"Shore! You do what you damn please," Barron thrust in, anxious to avoid any hitch. "What we want is results. That right, Mickle?"

Little as he liked the arrangement, Dunc was forced to acquiesce. "But we don't expect to pay you men and forget about you, either," he stipulated. "We want to know what you're doing. That's fair enough, isn't it?"

Robuck hesitated, then assented. With a few more words, the employment of he and his companions by the Association was settled.

"Well, what'll you do, now?" Barron asked, obviously pleased.

"We ought to know more about the situation than we do, for one thing. You say you've been having heavy losses," said Robuck, thinking aloud; "and they haven't been swallowin' those steers. First thing we do, we'll find out where they ship them."

Dale Barron found encouragement in this incisive brand of thinking. He answered questions exhaustively, and despite Dunc Mickle's noncommittal silence, was plainly willing to do everything he could to help. It was late when the conference broke up.

VIII: *The End of One Trail*

THE sun slanted diagonally across wild and broken land on the edge of the Blackfort Desert, draping the ledges and buttes with dusky shadows. It was late afternoon. Atop a crumbling, barren ridge sat two horsemen who, although they had just met, had ridden far. The dust of the desert trails powdered their faces and their clothes and lay thick on their stirrup fenders. They gazed steadily into the west.

"He said Friday," said Red Lefler, in a bothered tone; "just north of Black Butte. You don't reckon he's run into a tangle or somethin'?"

Deane shook his head. "It's half-an-hour till sundown. You know Bill. He'll be along."

Red, who was notoriously pessimistic when he "had the feelin'," complained lugubriously that something had gone plumb wrong for sure, when suddenly he straightened in the hull, at gaze. The sight of a rider a mile off across the waste, and jogging this way, made him forget what had been in his mind the moment before.

"There he comes now," he exclaimed triumphantly "I knew he'd make it on the dot! He always does!"

Jack's good-natured twitting over this change of front had no power to provoke him.

"Well, what about it?" he queried expectantly, as the three met. "Hit on anythin'?"

Robuck shook his head. "Not a thing," he admitted, a sober taciturnity in his mien.

Like his partners, he was grayed with the dust of travel, for he had ridden many miles since morning, and with no more success than had attended their joint efforts during the past ten days. It was increasingly evident that not thus would they find the tell-tale trail of rustled steers from the Flathead country. Nor, in this waterless and uninhabited desolation, had they met a single human.

"What about you two?" Robuck pursued, wiping his face with his sleeve. "Get any leads at all?"

"Nary a smell," Red replied.

More deliberately, Jack said: "I picked up the sign of five ponies, about noon. It led west from Dry Creek a few miles, then swung south. I lost it in the *malpais*."

"Shod ponies?"

"Yeah," said Jack. "Traveling fast, too."

They considered the information. It was their first inkling that Smoke Devlin's crowd might yet be holed up in this general vicinity; for since the train robbery no other sign of the outlaws' existence had been forthcoming.

"That don't get us nowhere," Red grumbled. "We combed that *malpais* from end to end."

"No," Robuck mused. "I'm afraid we'll have to crack this case another way."

"There's the railroads," Jack pointed out. "No telling what we might find out in some small shipping town."

Robuck nodded. "That's what I've been thinking, myself."

With many pauses for thought, he outlined the plan for their future investigations. Red he directed to return to Flathead, and, starting from a point fifty or sixty miles away, examine the small towns for another hundred miles along the main-line in either direction. He and Deane, he proceeded, would ride south to another railroad beyond the desert, there to pursue their inquiries.

"We'll meet you," he told Red, "in Twospot on the fifteenth. That's four days. If you find anything, pull out pronto and wait for us. And don't get tangled up with any roulette wheels."

Red grinned weakly.

They camped that night on a flat where a few spears of cured buffalo grass afforded browse for the horses. In the morning, Red was away before daylight. The rising sun found Robuck and Jack jogging south at an easy pace.

It was a hard day. The sun hammered them unmercifully from out of a brazen sky. Perspiration soaked and muddied the dust on the horses' barrels. There was an eerie silence over these interminable desert stretches which, Robuck at length confessed, had even him feeling creepy.

"It's as though someone were following us," he said, "and watching us—but you don't know where, or from what direction."

"I've had just the same feeling for two hours. More than that," Jack astonished him by adding, "it isn't an illusion."

"You mean someone is following us?" Robuck queried swiftly. "Have you seen anything?"

"No-o," Jack admitted. "But—" he resumed, as Robuck's features relaxed, "I'll lay you a boot-jack to a cigarette-paper that I'm right."

It could do no harm to relieve the iron monotony surrounding them with a little diversion. Robuck thought of it as nothing more. He said: "You prove that."

Deane nodded. A moment later he murmured: "Swing a little to the left. See that gap in the next ridge? We'll go through that—easy as ever, mind, and only a look or two around."

Robuck, smiling to himself, complied. Nearing the rocky cleft, Jack directed: "When you get through, pull off on your side, behind a rock, and don't make a sound."

The ponies clattered through the defile. On its far side, Robuck followed instructions, Jack doing the same. Waiting, their mounts at rest in the broiling sun, they hearkened to complete silence until Robuck began to grin. Suddenly, then, he sobered. The click of a hoof on rock drifted to him. His lean jaws hardened, a cold light springing into his eyes.

Who to expect he had no idea; but that did not primarily interest him. Men did not trail one another in desert country from benevolent motives. Everything he had learned of Smoke Devlin warned him the outlaw held a strangle-hold on the range for miles in every direction. His spies were everywhere. What more simple than to send a trusted rifleman into the desert after two cruising detectives, there to dispatch them with neatness and finality?

A rider emerged from the rocky defile, an alertness on him which snapped to tension as Robuck jumped his pony suddenly across his path. A rifle-stock jutted from his saddle boot and cartridge belts supported two sagging six-guns on his hips. But his only move, as his bronc came to a halt, was to cross his hands on the horn and ease his position in the saddle.

He was about forty, with a bleak, weather-bitten countenance which told nothing. His black eyes were perfect mirrors of opacity.

"Suppose you identify yourself, brother, and be damned quick about it!" Robuck snapped, his gun covering the other.

The man said flatly: "You're Robuck, aren't you—and Deane? . . . I'm Daggett."

"Is that supposed to mean anything to us?" Jack thrust in. "And while you're explainin', you better tell why you found it necessary to trail us."

Daggett's smile was slow. "I don't blame you boys for bein' suspicious. Me, I'm on the same job you are. Didn't Mickle say anythin' about the Association hirin' me, long before you come?"

As a matter of fact, Robuck did remember some mention of the man, a special investigator taken on at Dunc Mickle's suggestion.

"How do we know you're Daggett?"

The man had an identification card given him by the Association, for use in his contacts with the law. Moreover, his initials, D D, were carved in a dozen places about his equipment.

Robuck, for some reason, remained unsatisfied. "Why were you following us?" he sharply repeated.

Daggett made a deprecatory gesture. "Why wouldn't I be?" he countered smoothly. "I didn't know who you was till I got a good look. It's my job, same as yores, to know who folks are, and where they're headin', here on the Blackfoot."

It sounded reasonable. Robuck could detect no real flaw in the man's story. Yet for some reason, perhaps the look in his bland, secretive eyes, he distrusted him.

"You've got us figured now," he said shortly. "What about it?"

Daggett shrugged. "Another lead's pinched out, is all," he responded simply. He evinced slow indignation then. "You don't blame me for makin' shore, do you?" he demanded.

Robuck, thinking it over, answered only indirectly. "Okay," he nodded. "The best thing you can do is to clear out of here."

The other pulled his horse around with alacrity. "Standoffish cuss, ain't you?" he growled. "I shore will steer clear of you, if that's the way you feel about it!" Without delay, he jogged out of sight through the rocky gap.

Little was said for the next half-hour, as the two proceeded south. Finally Deane broke the silence to observe: "We might have got some information out of that bird, while we were at it."

"Noticed that, did you?" Robuck replied. "I told him he could go, just to see how he'd take it. You notice how quick he took me up . . . He didn't want to tell us anything," he added grimly.

"Glory hunter, eh?"

"I don't know. He's acting under Mickle's orders."

Despite a careful watch, they saw no more of Daggett. Late in the evening, they arrived at Deer Horn, a cowtown on the tin-pot branch railroad running west from Rocky Point.

The loading corrals were south of town. They rode down there, finding nothing of interest. Such inquiries as they made elicited no information of value. It was the old story over again. Smoking on the hotel porch after supper, they talked it over.

"Nothing down here for us," was Jack's conclusion. "Too much desert even for rustlers."

Robuck, however, was reluctant to give up. "There's a little town west of here—Salt Fork. We'll leave our horses here, ride up on the train tomorrow, and look it over," he proposed.

Jack commented sceptically that probably Salt Fork wasn't aware the Flathead country existed, but Robuck was firm. It was precisely because the towns along this railroad were entirely out of the sphere of knowledge of the Flathead country, he elaborated, that he had hopes of them.

Salt Fork, when they descended from the train the following morning, proved even smaller than they had been led to expect. A dozen sun-blackened buildings comprised the single street. The shipping pens were some distance apart; and they saw at once, from the cattle cars there, and the handful of men working near them, that someone was loading steers.

Disposing of their gear, they walked down. Rounding the corrals from the back, they managed to keep out of sight of the perspiring punchers at the chute. Jack, moving close, stared through the corral poles and exclaimed lowly:

"Look at that, Bill! Over-branded stock, every bit of it!"

It was true. There could be no doubt that the brands on these steers had been tampered with. After one swift glance, however, Robuck was asking himself who the men were who were loading the stuff, a tautness on him as he felt himself drawing nearer a solution to a puzzling problem.

A moment's scrutiny sufficed to confirm his suspicions. Two of the men across the corrals he did not know; but the third was Ike Geer.

Drawing swiftly back, Robuck grasped Jack's arm. "There's one of Smoke Devlin's men there," he muttered. "It cinches who's behind this. We'll find out who it is that turns the stuff over."

They turned away. Reaching the station, they routed out the agent.

"Who's shippin' the stuff in the loading pens" Robuck asked.

"Broke Horan," was the answer. Deane lifted his brows, but Robuck was not surprised.

"Does he load her often?"

"Yeah, he does." The agent, scrutinizing them, judged them to be punchers on the drift, looking for jobs. "Horan's up street some'eres, if you want to see him," he added carelessly.

"Thanks. We'll look for him there."

But Broke Horan was not there, when they went first to one, and then the other, of Salt Fork's two saloons. Nor was he in the general store. He was altogether too cagy a gent to be caught napping in this fashion. With the restless curiosity of his kind, he had observed them getting off the train. Stiffening, his pouchy face gray, he delayed only long enough to verify their identity, all his hatred of Robuck welling up afresh. He knew only too well what the other's presence in this town signified. When Robuck and his companion headed for the loading pens, Horan made his way hurriedly to the livery. Emerging a few minutes later, mounted on a rangy gray, he headed out of town at a brisk pace, with many a backward look.

Reaching the livery fifteen minutes later, Robuck and Jack found the place deserted. The swamper came across the street from the saloon, wiping his lips. He could tell them little. Sure, he knew Horan. Hadn't seen him for two-three hours, though.

Nodding thanks, they turned away. Before they had gone a dozen yards, the swamper called after them.

"Horan's bronc is gone," he said. "It was here, but he come and got it. Mebby they can tell you down to the loadin' chute where he's went to."

"Okay."

Robuck frowned. "That's that," he told Jack. "Either he got wind of us, or his business has taken him elsewhere. Our move now is to clamp down on those boys at the pens."

"What about the law?" Jack nodded toward the town marshal, eyeing them curiously from a doorway.

Robuck shrugged. "It'll be too late for him to horn in, by the time we've made our play."

Returning to the loading corrals by a round-about way, they looked over the ground. The three men were still busy prodding the steers aboard the cars. Dust billowed high in the air.

"I'll work around the pen," Jack proposed, "and we'll close in from each side. That ought to do it."

Robuck nodded. He had no thought of telling Deane what to do. Both were keyed up, with trouble as strong in their nostrils as the thick scent of dust. Neither had any idea that the men they sought to apprehended would give up without a fight.

Crouching low, the milling cattle in the pen concealing his movements, Jack stole away. Robuck delayed briefly, then started in the opposite direction. A dozen steps took him to the corner of the corral. He found himself in back of a man at the side of the chute, prodding through the slats.

For some moments this man worked steadily. Then something induced him to glance over his shoulder. Robuck was standing there, hands on hips; but the puncher found nothing innocuous in his presence. Whirling around with an oath, at the same instant he went for his gun without bothering to ask questions.

Only Robuck's shot ripped the afternoon, however. With a lightning draw, he sent a slug through the other's wrist, shattering the bones. The man let out a bellow. He dropped to his knees, grabbing for his fallen gun with the other hand. Springing forward, Robuck kicked it out of his reach.

Deane was equally busy. At the moment Robuck's shot cracked, a man clinging half-way up the chute glanced up to note Jack's approach. Plainly these men had been on the *qui-vive*. This one let go his hold on the chute with an astonishing wrench of his body, and dropped, going for his gun as he did so.

The gun roared. It jolted out of the rustler's grasp as he came down asprawl; he scrambled madly for it, Jack's snap-shot winging narrowly past his head. He recovered the gun—shot a second time, just as Deane flung himself aside. Then, a slug splashing dirt in his face, he flung himself under the cattle car.

The third rustler, Ike Geer, had suddenly disappeared. Jack gave him no thought then, darting around the end of the string and throwing a shot down the cars which persuaded the man underneath to change his mind about emerging on the far side. A gun pounded, back near the chute, which he guessed belonged to Robuck.

He was about to run down the side of the cars when a slight sound, apparently from overhead, caused him to throw a glance upward. He was in time to catch a flash of Ike Geer, standing on top of the car, his gun bearing directly on him. There was an evil glance on

Geer's visage, as though he meant physically to hurl the lead which would tear the life out of his victim.

Caught unawares, and losing his balance, Jack had no time to save himself. His breath sucked in with a gasp. Death stared him in the face and he looked back with a countenance of granite. Crashing backward, at the same instant he threw up his gun and let drive at the figure outlined against the sky.

Geer's shot smacked the ground near his face. Ike himself jerked erect, spun around like a dazed man, and spilled off the car-roof, to pile up on the ballast on one shoulder and the side of his head. Deane distinctly heard the dull snap of bones as he landed.

Jack ignored him, scrambling up. A shudder ran over him which he threw off. Down the cars a crawling figure drew his lead, which spatted against a car-truck. The man disappeared again.

"Lay off!" he bellowed, in an injured tone. "I got a bellyful, I tell yuh! I can't stand yuh both off. Lemme out of here!"

Jack advanced cautiously, ready for any trick. "Bill!" he called. "Everything all right?"

"Over here," was Robuck's response, from the other side of the car. "I got one of 'em."

Jack's relief was real, but his voice yet held a harsh rasp. "Show yourself, mister man," he told the rustler under the car. "And be mighty careful how you do it!"

The other complied, crawling out backwards. He stood up with his hands shoulder-high, while Jack went over him for weapons.

"Okay," grunted the latter. "Now step out nice and polite, while we join the others."

A moment later they reached Robuck and the rustler whose wrist had been smashed. The latter sat, groaning, against the side of the corral.

"What about Ike Geer?" queried Robuck swiftly. "Did he get away?"

"Geer's around by the first car," Jack told him grimly. "He'll keep."

Robuck nodded, a satisfied glint in his eyes. Except for Broke Horan, the round-up had been complete.

IX: *Tangling Trails*

THE marshal of Salt Fork came hurriedly down the siding, several men behind him. He had heard the ominous drum of gunfire. His cadaverous, mustached visage was portentous.

"What's the meanin' of this?" he demanded, as his eyes fell on the wounded rustler. "You fellers better explain yoreselves in a hurry!"

"We're stock detectives," Robuck told him, in an authoritative tone which had its effect. "These men were loading over-branded stock rustled from the Flathead country." Briefly he told his story, adding what had taken place here.

With the explanation, the marshal cooled considerably. Robuck and Deane's identification of themselves completed his deflation. Ordering Ike Geer's removal, he took the remaining pair of rustlers into custody.

Their hands free, Robuck and Jack turned to unloading the cattle cars. Half-an-hour sufficed to clear them. With the steers in the pens once more, Robuck turned them over to the marshal to hold. A few of the curious trailing after, he and Deane stepped to the station to explain to the agent and wire Flathead the news.

That done, they carried their saddles up to the livery barn. The awed swamper rented them the best ponies in the corral. Before noon they were riding out of town.

Broke Horan had taken no pains to cover his tracks, so hasty had been his departure. In ten minutes they picked up his sign and swung in behind him. Jack was for pushing briskly forward, but Robuck said no.

"He may have a good three hours' start on us," he pointed out. "We could burn out these broncs without ever seeing his dust . . . If we stick to his trail, that's enough. He'll be at the end of it."

All afternoon they rode through the sere and frowning desert without seeing any sign of life other than the sunning lizards. Horan was striking straight north. Only insurmountable obstacles caused him to deviate from his course. More than once, when the scarified rock left no trace of his passing, they picked up his tracks a mile or two farther on.

"You might say, from the way he's riding," said Jack, "that he hasn't a thing in the world to worry him. *I* think he's so plumb rattled that he can't see an inch beyond his nose."

"You mean he saw us and ran," supplied Robuck. "We'll find out, when he commences to think."

"He hasn't forgotten what you did to him," Jack proceeded; "and he isn't likely to forget what you'll do to him next time. That's the spur that's drivin' him now. Question is, where to?"

"He'll see that word gets to Smoke Devlin. But not even Horan would get so rattled that he'd lead us right to Smoke's hideout," was Robuck's opinion.

Horan's trail led on into the sunset, penetrating

deeper and deeper the Blackfoot Desert. With the onset of darkness they were forced to pull up, strong as was the impulse to push on.

"I've had an eye on Horan from the minute I knew he was friendly with Buff Ogle—but we know for certain what he's up to now," said Robuck. "There's no sense in throwin' away our one chance of nailin' him. If we lose him now, Lord knows when we'll catch up with him again."

They put in such a night as had often been their lot, chafing under the knowledge that darkness need not stop their quarry; that in all probability he was steadily increasing the distance between himself and them. With the first pink streamers of dawn they were in the saddle again.

That day they found a change in the character of the trail they followed. Horan had indeed begun to think, his actions showing a shrewdness which harked back to a time when he had been a better man. His course began to wind back and forth, following the rocky patches, seeking rather than avoiding the rough going. At times they had nothing but shoe scratches on granite or lava by which to trace his progress.

It took time. They found themselves advancing slower than a man might walk a horse. Robuck, who had felt his grasp closing on the cattle buyer, grew brusque of movement and terse in his answers. He clung to the trail with iron persistence.

The climax came when it faded out altogether. They hunted for an hour before admitting defeat. But that conclusion was inevitable—Broke Horan might have taken wing and flown, for all the evidence he left of his going.

"There's no doubt that he knew we were after him," Robuck confirmed Jack's views. "Which means that he'll think twice before showing himself in town, where we could easily pick him up. He'll go straight to Smoke Devlin—and that leaves us right where we were before."

They decided, since they were within a few hours of there, to strike for Flathead.

Riding out of the desert into habitable range, they crossed creeks and threaded thinly wooded ridges. While they continued to inspect closely such sign as they came on, they saw nothing of interest.

Could they have seen the rider who emerged from the trees on a wooded bench a moment after they passed, they would have changed their minds in a hurry. This man's eye fell on them and swiftly narrowed. Lafe Rash, who had escaped from the courthouse in Wagonspoke, miles to the south in another state, had watched this pair too closely in the past to be mistaken about them now. A glimpse of Robuck's lean face, as he turned his head to speak to Deane, left his identity unquestioned.

Lafe drew back into the trees, the hand of fear suddenly clutching him in its icy grip. Why were these men here, where he had made sure they would never overtake him? Were they on his trail? The thought went through him like the turn of a knife. With a fierce gesture, he half-drew the rifle from his saddle-boot.

"I can do it!" he told himself in a savage whisper.

"Put a slug in them gents, and the trail ends right here! God knows I've got enough to square with 'em!"

They disappeared from view; and so unwarning had been their appearance that it might have been an illusion. Wheeling hastily, Rash threaded the trees until he came out again at a point where the two were under his eye. This time his rifle was in his hands, and those hands trembled.

The temptation was great. No one had seen him in this country except a nester or two. He had kept away from towns; not from design, for he had long since considered himself reasonably safe, but because it had happened that way.

Robuck, he decided, was no longer on his trail. Detectives rarely followed a rustler from one state to another. Robuck was on another job; he wasn't even aware of Rash's presence. It would be easy to take advantage of the situation, and then ride out of the country. No one would ever know.

But Rash, for all the fierce hatred of Robuck which heated his veins, was not beyond caution. He had good and sufficient reason to remember the potentialities of these men. He didn't trust himself to get them both, even from ambush. The odds were too great.

"But that don't mean it'll end this way!" he ground out, as his rifle came down. His gaunt, swarthy face darkened with wrath—anger against Robuck for having unleashed the hounds of fear at his heels once more. "I'll settle with him one way or another, if I have to stick here till I do it!"

Red Lefler was happy today; happier than he had been in some time. The fact that he was ravenously hungry was the only cloud on his horizon. As he jogged along, humming a tuneless sing-song, he wished that he carried coffee with him, as Jack Deane did. But when he was where he could get it, he drank plenty, and forgot that he'd be likely to want more later. This was rather complicated to get straight, and Red was frowning over it when sight of a cluster of buildings ahead brought him out of his revery.

Five minutes later he drew up before the tumble-down hotel at Elk Crossing. HANK'S PLACE, the sign read. Across the way stood a store, also run by Hank. Sheds made up the balance of Elk Crossing.

He found young Sam Barron in the hotel dining-room, about to partake of a meal along with several sour-looking individuals.

"Howdy, Lefler," the boy greeted. "Ain't lost out here, are you?"

Red said he had taken a little ride. He was all done now, and on his way back to Flathead. "Seen anythin' of my partners, lately?" he asked.

Sam hadn't. His opinion of Bill Robuck, however, was excellent. He had much to say about the fight Robuck had taken off his hands a fortnight ago, to which Red listened good-naturedly. They were getting acquainted in great style, without neglecting their meal, when a sharp clatter of hoofs outside drew their eyes to the door.

"Some outfit with money in their pants, spoilin' for

fun," Red hazarded, as stamping ponies drew up before the hotel.

But something told him that all was not as it should be, as the mounted men, harder-looking than any cow outfit, leaned forward in the saddle to peer in at the windows. His suspicion was confirmed when, without warning, a gun crashed and the slug, carrying away a window-pane and part of the sash, smashed a bottle on the table.

"That's Smoke Devlin out there!" Sam Barron cried, his voice rising sharply.

With the exception of Sam and Red, the diners dived for cover without awaiting confirmation. Red sprang to his feet, a wolfish expression on his face. Whipping out his gun, he opened fire as the outlaws outside made a rush for the door.

It deterred them only momentarily. Hugging windows and door, they searched the room with a gust of lead. Red and Sam hunkered behind an overturned table, replying more deliberately.

"They're after me!" Red told the boy harshly. "No need of you takin' a hand in this. Crawl out the back way and leg it. You kin git away!"

Sam whirled on him fiercely. "Where d'you get that stuff? They're smokin' me, same as you! I'm stickin'!"

Red's big hand closed on his arm, drawing him close. Burning eyes stared straight into his own.

"Don't be a fool! Those hombres out there are curly wolves! We're cornered like rats in a trap—you don't want to die!"

Sam jerked himself free. "Forget it!" he advised

hardily. "I'm in this whether I like it or not. And I like it!" He whipped a shot at the window as splinters sprang from the table, showering them both.

Red would have flung him bodily toward safety. On the instant, however, the outlaws attempted once more to storm the door. Red got a flash of Smoke Devlin's craggy face. The pound of six-guns rocked the room like a string of blasts. Vinegar and catsup bottles sprang into a thousand bits; a coffee pot clattered to the floor.

Powdersmoke hazed the room so thickly that seeing was difficult; but hugging their narrow bulwark when the savage flurry was over, the defenders were uncomfortably aware that one of the outlaws had won to a position inside the room with them. It was Roy Olds. His slugs ripped up the floor, smacked the wall at their backs.

"Get him!" Sam grated, cautiously hunting an exposed elbow or knee to target. But instead, at a crashing shot, Sam himself suddenly jerked up and then sprawled out laxly.

"My Gawd!" Red tried to rouse him. "Did you git hit bad?"

Sam made no answer. Turning away, Red nodded to himself. He knew what he was facing. It would go on like this, the outlaws gaining inch by inch, drawing the net tighter around him until, with a last vicious burst of gunfire, they wiped him out. His long lips only tightened at the prospect, his eyes crinkling to fearless ice.

Harsh cries sounded without. Devlin's men made another rush, their guns spitting. Red hugged the riddled table, a hail of slugs slapping around him; firing coolly, but knowing himself hopelessly out-numbered.

"This is the finish!" he muttered grimly, determined to sell his life as dearly as possible.

At that moment, yells and the quick rap of boot-heels rang out from behind him. In less than the flicker of an eye Red swung his gun around—and held his unerring fire in the nick of time, as an anxious yell struck through his absorption.

"Red! Where are you?"

It was Jack Deane. Robuck was at his shoulder. They burst through the rear door, guns thundering as the figures of Devlin and his men darkened the outer door and windows. Red rose with a savage cry on his lips, a cry of triumph. With these men at his side, he felt himself invulnerable.

For a blazing moment, death swept the place on leaden wings. The outlaws hung on, met by an unexpected defiance, but seeing their victim slip through their fingers. At a wrathy bellow from Devlin, they abruptly fell back.

Pressing the advantage, the trio sprang forward. As they did so, Roy Olds straightened up in the far corner, a snarl on his lips. He made no attempt to run, fire spurting from his waist. Robuck cut him down without the slightest compunction, sending a slug smashing through his head.

They reached the door. The outlaws were swinging into the saddle, fury in their twisted visages. Several of them had been hit. Blood streamed from the fingers of Buff Ogle's hand; another clutched a stained shoulder. A savage fusillade covered their sweeping start. Dashing around the corner of the hotel, they were gone from sight.

Red turned back inside without delay. "Young Barron's in here," he said. "Dunno whether he's done for or not."

A slug had furrowed Sam's head. They worked over him for some minutes before he came to. He staggered up just as Hank Blascom, the proprietor, sure the hostilities were over, stormed in with belated authority.

"What in hell's goin' on here?" he demanded. "Yuh don't hafta pick my hotel for yore battles!" He was a gross, mean-faced man.

Robuck silenced him with a word or two. Blascom, still indignant, turned to the task of carrying the dead outlaw outside and setting his place to rights.

Robuck, thinking that they were speedily squaring matters with Smoke Devlin for the robbery of the bullion train, turned to Red. "Suppose you tell us what this is all about," he invited.

"Devlin musta trailed me here," Red responded, ruefully. "I fell over his hideout this mornin'. I swear I didn't know he spotted me. I watched his bunch movin' around this dugout in the side of a wash. There ain't no doubt about who they were. Later a feller rode away alone, and I dogged him—"

"Who?" Robuck put in.

"Some oldtimer I've seen around Flathead. Dunno his name—yes I do, too. It's Poke—Pork—Spokey! That's it! Spokey Withers."

They knew who he meant. "What happened then?" Robuck pursued.

Red had followed Spokey for some miles, and finally lost him. Knowing better than to go back and tackle Devlin's crowd single-handed, and determining to put his information in Robuck's possession as soon as possible, he had headed for Flathead. At Elk Crossing he stopped for a meal, fell in with Sam Barron—and they knew the rest.

"If Devlin got wise and follered me here, he won't go back to that dugout, though," Red concluded gloomily.

"No, that's out," Robuck agreed. "Thing for us to do now is to get Sam home."

But as they made ready to ride, Jack Deane was far from satisfied to let the matter drop, his thoughts circling persistently around Spokey Withers, whom Red had seen riding away from Smoke Devlin's hidden dugout. It meant little to the others, except that Spokey was a member of the gang. But Deane, remembering the night he had seen the man in conference with Dunc Mickle at the Flathead bank, felt he knew something they did not. Did it mean that some connection existed between the banker and Smoke Devlin? Maybe it didn't; but it certainly was something to think about.

Could he have been present at the meeting which took place in the bank that evening, he would have entertained no more doubts. Mickle had been expecting Spokey, and was behind his desk when the latter's knock came. He let him in.

"Dunc, you gotta do somethin' about these three stock detectives!" Spokey opened up. "I ain't the only one that thinks so, neither!"

"Suppose you lower your voice," Mickle told him severely. "Now—tell me what this is about."

Spokey was in no wise abashed. A harsh immediacy in his manner, he told how the detectives had come within an ace of laying hands on Broke Horan, and how the cattle buyer felt about it.

"Besides that," he pursued, "they split up, and that red-headed jasper stumbled onto Smoke's hideout this mornin'. He watched me ride away. I give him the slip, tipped off Smoke, and Smoke and the boys went whoopin' after him." He described the results of the fight at Elk Crossing. "Olds is the second one them birds've rubbed out now. Smoke like to busted a cinch—he's plumb riled! He says for you to get rid of them three, and be damned quick about it!" Spokey's voice held an unaccustomed ring. "Don't make no mistake about this, Dunc," he warned. "Smoke means what he says!"

Mickle scowled throughout the narrative, his glance smoldering. "I told Daggett to keep an eye on those men," he rapped out. "Where was he?"

"I don't know."

Dunc drummed on the desk. There was no doubt in his mind as to the seriousness of the situation. "I'll take care of the detectives," he grunted. "I can't fire them now. Folks would think it was queer. All I can do is to discredit them—make them look so sick they'll quit. But you can tell Devlin I'll keep them together, and they'll take my orders, too!"

He thought a moment, his eyes narrowing. His head came up. "They'll be here tomorrow," he mused thoughtfully. "Tell you what you do: Go out to my S C ranch. Tell Rawlins to drive a bunch of steers into the hills and cache 'em. Then he's to bust into town with news of a raid. I'll send Robuck and his friends out there—and see to it, this time, that Daggett keeps an eye on them!

"In the meantime," he continued, "let Devlin know how it stacks up. He's to go after the Cross 8, tomorrow night, without any interference. Tell him," Mickle directed, his voice grating, "to sink the hooks in, there, deep! . . . Will that do it?" He leaned back in the swivel-chair, pleased with his scheme.

"Sounds all right," Spokey nodded. But he was plainly unconvinced. They talked over each point of the plan, ironing out the kinks. When they were done, Mickle was satisfied that it could not fail to produce the desired results.

"Maybe this'll pay Barron out, too," he commented, his lean face dark and cold. "He's the one who saddled those detectives on us. You might remind Smoke Devlin of that!"

X: *Bushwhack Lead*

SAM BARRON felt pretty good on leaving Elk Crossing for his father's ranch; he even wanted to talk about that part of the fight which he had missed. Before he had ridden far, however, reaction set in. The blood left his face. He felt so weak that he couldn't hang on, and would have crashed out of the saddle had not Red been close enough to catch him.

They let him rest awhile, but the shock of his wound proved severe. When they reached the Cross 8 late in the afternoon, Red was carrying the boy across his saddle-bow.

The Barron ranch was a sizeable place, built on a flat beside Willow Creek. A welter of corrals and outbuildings clustered behind the house. It was a ranch that looked like, and was, a home.

Sam was soon tucked in bed, his sister's and his father's fears for him allayed. Dorrie, the grumpy but capable housekeeper who took charge of him, said that a night's rest would work wonders.

Dale Barron herded Robuck, Jack and Red into the living-room and, scarcely waiting for their story, embarrassed them with voluble appreciation. He knew about the stock they had recovered at Salt Fork; some of those steers had been rustled from his range.

"You've done more than anyone else has been able

to do," he told them warmly. "I feel proud of pickin' you for the job. There ain't no question but what you'll go on to a clean finish."

He left no doubt, either, of his belief that their uncovering of Broke Horan's activities, despite the buyer's escape, would materially embarrass the rustlers in disposing of stolen cattle. But when he learned about Red Lefler's discovery of the outlaw's hideout, and the fight at Elk Crossing, resulting in the death of a second member of the gang, his approval knew no bounds.

"By golly, that's fine!" he ejaculated, his ruddy face beaming. "If you can't get rid of them skunks no other way, you can wipe 'em out! They deserve all they get, and you won't hear a peep out of me!"

Red alone basked in this reflected glory. His pleasure was genuine: He had taken a liking to young Sam; he liked his father's bluff and hearty manner. An infectious smile overspreading his rawboned, homely features, he signified his entire willingness to discuss events over a cigar.

Robuck and Jack were glad to escape to the porch with Virginia, whose simple and friendly manner readily put them at their ease.

"I am particularly glad of your success at Salt Fork, because of its effect on Father," she told them. "It means the breaking of the blank wall of hopelessness this rustling has presented."

"We couldn't help noticing," Robuck assented. "He seems enormously relieved. Has the rustling been getting into him as bad as that?"

"Yes, it has—especially since it came at a bad time," the girl explained. She seemed reluctant, but entirely frank. "You see, when the price of beef dropped to nothing four years ago, Father was forced to mortgage the ranch. Since the rustling began, he has found it increasingly difficult to meet his payments, although the —mortgagor has been decidedly pressing."

"That's a shame," Jack sympathized gruffly.

"Yes. And not only that," she continued; "but Mr. Mickle has also been urging Father to sell him the ranch. It all adds up to an extremely trying situation."

"Do I understand," Robuck queried carefully, "that it is Mickle who holds the mortgage?"

She looked at him in surprise, but admitted that such was the case.

For his part, Deane was mentally biting his lips in some vexation. It did not escape him that although he put in an occasional word, it was to Robuck that Virginia raised her eyes—him to whom she directed her words. Not even the interest Jack found in this further illumination of the character of Dunc Mickle caused him to overlook the girl's unconscious bestowal of favor upon his partner.

"I don't suppose your father has any intention of selling," Robuck proceeded, watching the play of expression in her face and her warm brown eyes. He was more absorbed by this than he would have cared to admit.

"Of course not," she agreed. A pensiveness came over her then. "As long as it doesn't come to a point where he is forced to," she amended.

He knew from that that her father's situation was even worse than she had said.

"What can Mickle's particular interest be in the Cross 8?" he inquired.

"You have no doubt learned," she replied, "that he already owns three ranches. They all lie on this side of Flathead—his S C ranch is only fifteen miles from here . . . Because of Father's water-rights, the Cross 8 controls range expansion in this vicinity."

"I see."

It was the age-old struggle for strategic position, which men called business.

The talk turned to other things. Jack, irked by an isolation which he felt keenly, chafed to get away. When Dale Barron and Red emerged to join them, he proposed a start for Flathead. Barron wouldn't hear of it.

"After what you boys've done for me?" he rumbled. "Not a bit of it! You'll stay here tonight. Take it easy. Am I right?" he demanded bluntly, swinging on Robuck.

"Why—" Robuck began.

"Sure," Red put in hastily. "We kin go on to town in the mornin'." He foresaw a pleasant evening divided between this cordial rancher and the punchers in the bunkhouse, and wanted nothing to stand between.

The truth was, Robuck was himself content to remain near this glowing girl who had grown in an astonishingly short time to mean so much in his inner thoughts.

They ate supper at the house—a pleasant meal,

Barron doing everything in his power to make them satisfied with the country and with their position. Dorrie reported Sam to be feeling better, and asking for food. After the meal, Red went in to talk to him. His father cornered Deane in the living-room, and Robuck found himself and Virginia free to do what they would.

They returned to the porch, the pair of them. Night had fallen; a half-moon rode in the velvet sky, silvering the range.

"I suppose it is unusual for you to spend an evening in this fashion," said Virginia, as they enjoyed the quiet peace.

Robuck smiled. "We spend a good many nights in the open. Ordinarily we're intent on something besides the night," he admitted.

Gradually she got him to talk of his experiences. If he was inclined to make the apprehension of criminals a tame-sounding affair, she readily supplied the seasoning of danger and personal prowess which he omitted.

Later, animated by some restlessness, the cause of which neither wholly understood, they left the porch to stroll in the yard. Robuck, conscious of the disturbing nearness of this girl, was evoking her soft and merry laughter with one of Red Lefler's ridiculous escapades, when suddenly he stiffened.

"What is it?" she queried, as he remained motionless, staring across the yard.

He had spotted someone skulking between the ranch

buildings in such a manner as to indicate that he had no right there.

"What will you do?" she whispered tensely. "Perhaps Father—or the men—" It was in the minds of both that this might mean some form of retaliation for the fight at Elk Crossing.

"No." Robuck was terse, laying a warning hand on her arm. "Go back to the house and remain quiet until I see who this is." He sounded more reassuring and cool than he really was.

"Be careful!" she breathed, as he left her side.

Dropping his cigarette, he stole forward. The flooding moonlight made it possible to see in the open with some clearness, but it was the tangle of shadows around the barn, the sheds and the corrals, that he sought to probe, his hand hovering near his gun.

Whoever he had seen, seemed to have faded in thin air. He frowned, however, as he glanced back to see the girl standing where he had left her. There was an independence, a trim assurance about her slight form which made him suck in his breath sharply at thought of her being cut down by a rifle in the hands of some merciless skulker.

When it came, however, the orange stab of gunfire was directed at himself. It licked the night with alarming suddenness. Robuck felt the wicked flutter of the slug past his face. Hot resentment surged up in him; without thought of his own safety, he sprang toward the spot from whence the shot had been fired, a leaping hand dragging his six-gun out.

No concrete antagonist awaited him in the gloom;

only the thick feeling of menace, and after a freighted moment, the quickening slap of running feet, drawing away. He plunged after. Breaking through between two sheds, he was in time to get a flash of a man springing into the saddle across the corrals. He snapped a shot over there, apparently without effect. The pony whirled and leaped away, its rider crouched low over its neck. In a moment, nothing but the diminuendo of retreating hoofs came back.

Thrasping away through the deceptive brush, Lafe Rash cursed himself for his clumsiness. A clean chance —and he had muffed it! Enraged to the point of frenzy by his failure, he redoubled his determination to mete out the vengeance which, in his mind, Robuck so richly deserved.

Attracted by the shots, Deane, Red, Dale Barron, his foreman and a number of punchers came on the run. In a few words Robuck explained what had happened.

"That's bad!" the rancher scowled. "You ain't got any idea who it was?"

"Not from seeing him—no," Robuck replied.

The matter was discussed at length, but there was no more to be learned. At a late hour, Robuck and his partners turned in at the bunkhouse. They were up the next morning with the punchers. The rising sun found them on their way to Flathead.

Reaching town shortly after nine o'clock, they went at once to the bank. Mickle received them in his usual dry manner.

Robuck gave a detailed account of all that had taken

place. He was at a loss to account for the evident dissatisfaction with which Mickle received it. Deane, however, asking himself how the banker would take all this, wondered if Dunc's behavior did not fit in with the suspicions slowly taking form in his mind.

"Don't run away with the idea that you've cracked this rustlin' situation," Mickle told Robuck, giving him the benefit of his inscrutable glance. "I don't think you have."

"Why not?" Robuck queried, brought up short. "You'd say things look better than they did, wouldn't you?"

"Well—not much." Mickle was deliberate. "You recovered a handful of steers, and what else does it amount to? Those prisoners don't amount to a thing. A jury will free them in less than an hour. If you'd done what you set out to," he added, with critical bluntness, "you'd have grabbed this Horan."

"I've explained how it happened that we lost him," said Robuck, with some warmth. "It simply couldn't be helped."

"Don't try to cover up," Dunc warned him smugly. "I can read the situation right from here. If you boys had stuck together, you wouldn't have bungled the thing," he added with conviction.

"If we'd stuck together," Robuck retorted, "Red never would have turned up Smoke Devlin's hideout!"

"What good did that do?" Dunc countered, as quickly. "He nearly succeeded in gettin' himself killed, and that's all."

Ordinarily, at such a time, Jack would have had something to say. Now he held his peace, following the trend of Mickle's subtle discrediting of their efforts with considerable interest. Red, on the other hand, was getting rapidly steamed up. He had accepted Dale Barron's compliments at face value; to have the banker reverse the decision in this summary fashion was more than he could swallow.

"You sound 's if you wisht I had got myself killed, and been done with it," he told Mickle tartly. "Don't you want us to turn up these buzzards and smoke 'em out?"

"You've mistaken my reason for hirin' you," Dunc responded blandly, "if you entertain the notion I don't! It's a question of methods." He measured them all with thinly concealed arrogance before he proceeded. "I'm not tellin' you boys where to head in," he reminded; "but after this, do as I say, and stay together. With the crooked element in this community what it is, you won't get nowheres any other way."

"What can it matter how we do our work, so long as we get it done?" Robuck rapped out. His patience with what he believed simply to be more than usually troublesome officiousness was short.

But Jack Deane was fitting another spoke in the wheel which bade fair in the end to roll away with Dunc Mickle. "Insists on us stickin' together," he mused inwardly. "That wouldn't be because he wants to know what we're up to, maybe?"

"Don't give me no arguments," said Mickle dogmatically, presenting a flinty front to Robuck. "I know what's best, no matter what you think about it . . . If you'd been together," he added craftily, "when you stumbled over this outlaw den, there might've been a different story to tell."

"That's possible," Robuck admitted thoughtfully. "More than that, it helps me to make up my mind." His lifting glance was level. "Mickle, if you'll give me half-a-dozen men, I believe I can run Smoke Devlin out of the country."

Dunc showed his first flash of fire. His lean cheeks darkened; his words were forceful.

"Poppycock! A posse? That'd be clever, wouldn't it?" His stare was scornful. "Surely you don't expect to find Devlin where you found him before? Dashin' around through the hills with a bunch of men would be the surest way there is of advertisin' yourself!" He snorted harshly, managing to look both disgusted and bored.

Deane, however, read the tinge of anxiety beneath his vehemence. The conviction that Mickle was secretly protecting Smoke Devlin grew on him steadily.

"No," Dunc continued; "you go on the way you've been doin'. I don't want to hear no more about a posse. Folks'd begin to talk, if we tried such a thing. They'd say you couldn't do your work—and we don't want that." So, adroitly, he put over the impression that it was not his objection alone which ruled out the idea of a posse.

Red growled his disgruntlement, staring at Mickle with amazed distaste. Robuck, accustomed to dealing with stubborn men, argued as patiently as he could.

But Dunc was not to be moved. His matter-of-fact dryness and unwavering eye gave the impression that he had made up his mind; that here was a man whose seasoned decisions were final. He even appeared so sure he was right as to be willing to humor Robuck, at far as words went at least. They were still deep in discussion when Mickle glanced up from his desk at a clatter of hoofs in the street outside the bank, and the hasty entrance of an excited man. Seeing Mickle, the man headed for him without ceremony.

"Well, Rawlins?" Dunc was wearing his best not-to-be-disturbed manner.

"Dunc—this is somethin' that can't wait!" Rawlins burst out, lowering his voice out of deference to the dignity of the bank, but without relaxing in insistence. "These yore Association detectives? Reckon they'll be interested, too."

"Tell it," Dunc directed shortly.

Rawlins lost little time. He was, they learned, Mickle's foreman in charge of the S C ranch. During the night, rustlers had raided the herd, getting away with a bunch of steers.

"Happened I was on the range at the time," Rawlins told them. "I seen 'em at work and rode up on 'em. They hazed the beef toward Feather Creek. When they got across, they opened up on me."

"So you let 'em get clean away?" Mickle snapped.

Rawlins protested: "Dunc, what could I do? I didn't have nobody with me! My bronc got a graze as it was. Sleepy'll tell you—"

"Never mind," Dunc cut him off. "Give us the rest of it!"

Seeing himself outnumbered, Rawlins had gone for the S C men. When they got back to the creek no trace of the rustlers was to be found. They had pushed on, combing the hlils with frantic haste until dawn disclosed the fact that they had found nothing, perhaps would find nothing. Rawlins had immediately got up a fresh horse and started for Flathead to report.

There was more of this. When he had elicited all the facts available, Mickle turned to Robuck, his manner short.

"You better get out there," he said. "Don't lose no time about it—and see if you can get some results this time."

Robuck, like Red, had been caught up in the tension of this latest raid. Smoke Devlin was certainly bearing down hard, for all the pressure they had brought to bear on him. It warned Robuck that the outlaw was ready to meet him on any grounds, and that, even as Mickle had said, they still had a hard fight ahead of them.

"We'll get started right away," he nodded, glancing significantly at his partners. Red was straining at the leash, his alert countenance craggy; but as they turned away with Rawlins, Jack bent a thoughtful glance on Dunc Mickle which would have set that worthy to thinking had he observed it.

XI: *False Scent and True*

DUNC MICKLE'S S C ranch lay spread across tumbled and brush-covered range far from easy to comb. Robuck, Jack and Red rode in ever-widening, bisecting arcs, in the direction in which Rawlins said the rustled steers had been driven. The foreman himself sided first one, then another of them, still voluble with his story.

"Wisht he'd hogtie that dang tongue of his," Red muttered disgustedly to Robuck, meeting the latter in the brush. "There's so much chatter rattlin' outa him, a feller can't hear himself think."

Robuck nodded absently. The same thought had been in his own mind. But nothing could hold his attention for long when there lay before him a tangled rustlers' trail to unravel.

The S C crew, working far beyond the ranch on open range, had little to offer in the way of information. They had not even succeeded in sticking to the trail of the stolen stock.

Early in the afternoon, one of them rode up to say that he'd picked it up again. From the direction he pointed out, Robuck's keen sleuthing instinct told him the puncher was mistaken; but he sent Red with the man to make sure.

They rode for half-an-hour through broken hills

without finding anything but the week-old tracks of single steers. The puncher looked puzzled at first, then sheepish.

"Danged if I ain't lost it again," he mumbled. "But I did see it!" he hastened to insist, stubbornly. "Place where a dozen steers dangled along, good an' plain."

"What yuh mean?" Red caught him up sceptically. "Didn't it look's if they'd been foggin' it?"

Thinking a minute, the puncher shook his head decidedly. "Can't say's it did. They seemed to be spraddled out an' givin' trouble, but not in no sweat."

"Any pony tracks?" Red pressed on.

"Well . . . I noticed one set."

As puzzled as his informant, Red scratched his head. When it became apparent they were not going to locate what they sought, he made a quick decision. Turning his pony, he started away.

"Where you goin'?" the puncher called.

"Back," Red told him succinctly. Without waiting for the other's indignant protest, he spurred on.

Robuck, when Red told him the upshot of the matter, a moment later, thought it over musingly, his eyes slitted as he gazed in the direction Red and the puncher had gone.

"Not a blame thing over there, near's I could see," the red-headed one grunted. "Yuh don't s'pose that was a try at tollin' us off, or somethin'?"

Robuck demurred. "No point in that," he said. And after a moment, thoughtfully: "Didn't Rawlins say he picked up that puncher off the grubline a couple weeks ago?"

"Yeah . . . What you thinkin' about, Bill?"

"He don't know this range so good," Robuck responded; "and he's got nothing to gain or lose in this . . . What I'm getting at is that I believe him."

Red stared in perplexed surprise. "Bill, I told you he didn't locate a thing over there!" he protested. "And when I heard that horraw story about the rustled stuff bein' walked—"

"Never mind," Robuck cut him off. "Get Jack and bring him along. We're going over there and take a good look."

He could scarcely have justified his decision by argument; yet to his trained ear the puncher's story, despite his lack of proof, possessed an air of reality that transcended invention.

With half-an-hour they were combing the range in the new direction. Time passed, and they met with no more success than before. It was Robuck who, mounting a hogback to scan their surroundings, located the beaten trail of steers there, instead of in the hidden washes and coulees they had been following. He waved the others to him. In silence they regarded this evidence that the puncher had been right. At this point, the steers had been hazed along in a lively fashion, and there was no telling how many men had been driving them; but that they were the missing steers appeared unquestionable.

"By golly, now we're gittin' somewheres!" Rawlins declared, with a show of enthusiasm. Where before he had been gloomily pessimistic, he became noisily cheerful.

"Lordy! What a pest," Red grumbled to himself.

A couple of miles farther on, they came suddenly upon a deep gully carved in the range, the existence of which, from a hundred yards' distance, might never have been guessed. Below them, as they followed the cattle tracks to the edge of the gully, they saw a brush corral, concealed cunningly—but not so cunningly that they did not instantly note its contents. Upward of a dozen steers stood in the enclosure, droop-headed in the downbeating sun. Robuck stared unbelievingly for a second, before rapping out low words:

"Get back! Somebody'll be standing guard. We don't want to pack any slugs away from here!"

Hastily backing away, they flung a loose net around the gully. Under Robuck's motioned directions, they closed in, guns at the ready.

No warning shot broke the slumbering silence as they slid into the gully and converged on the brush corral. No scuttling figure broke for cover. The gully was deserted except for themselves.

"My stuff, all right!" Rawlins burst out exultantly. Riding near, he ran his eye over the flank-branded S C steers. Suddenly he was indignant. "Dang their lousy hides!" he ripped out. "They run beef off these cows—an' then left 'em without water!" He fumed on, muttering.

"They didn't get very far," Deane remarked. "This can't be more than twelve or fifteen miles from your home range."

"That's right," Rawlins discovered, gazing blankly.

"My boys must've been pretty close to 'em. They couldn't get the stuff away."

Robuck said nothing.

A circle a mile in circumference drawn around the spot failed to turn up any sign of the departed rustlers. Breaking down the corral, they hazed the steers out of the gully and started them back toward the S C range.

On the return trip, Rawlins was more talkative than ever. Then, abruptly, he fell silent. Red looked at him in surprise. When at length Rawlins spoke again, it was to grumble: "I should think you fellers'd make a harder stab'n you did at snaggin' them rustlers. You didn't hardly look at all."

"We looked hard enough to tell us what we were already pretty sure of," Robuck replied. "If those men had to get out in a hurry, they weren't leaving any sign-boards to point out their direction."

"Wal, you're trailers, ain't yuh?" Rawlins demanded shrewdly.

Red laughed at him. "Sure. In two days we'd guarantee to trail them birds right to the stage-road from Flathead to Twospot. And then what?"

Rawlins dropped the subject. Reaching the S C in late afternoon, he suggested that they stop over. He even pressed his invitation, holding out the usual range inducements. But they refused.

"We'll amble along," said Robuck.

"What's the hurry?" Rawlins insisted. "You done what you could. Might's well take it easy till next time."

Robuck shook his head decidedly, finding a part of his inducement to go on in the fact that the Barron ranch lay on their way back to town. Reading this without difficulty, Jack Deane made no comment. They had all had enough of Rawlins' not very pleasant personality.

They left shortly, riding along abreast. A mile away from the S C, Red broke the reflective silence to ask: "What's on your mind, Bill?"

Robuck, weighing his reply, said deliberately: "Those steers were never rustled."

"Wha-at?" Red was amazed. "What makes you think that?"

"According to the story," Robuck pointed out, "the rustlers had five or six hours of the best time, from midnight on—yet they only drove the steers that far. How does it look to you?"

"You can't tell what rustlers are likely to do," Deane put in reasonably.

"Furthermore," Robuck continued steadily, "if you saw what I did, you noticed there wasn't a crumb of mud on those steers' hocks."

"What's 'at got to do with it?" Red demanded, mystified.

"Think back," Robuck grinned. "Rawlins said what? That he *saw* those rustlers haze the steers across Feather Creek. Am I right?"

"Gee! Yeah—" Red admitted.

"I don't believe him," said Robuck flatly. "That stock was driven up across the flats, the same way we drove it back. It was never anywhere near Feather Creek."

"Red's expression of bewilderment was comical. "Why'd anybody give us the run-around like that?" he puzzled.

"Maybe," Robuck answered soberly, "while we were out there, something's been going wrong somewhere else."

Jack was eyeing him thoughtfully, more interested than the others could have guessed. "You may be right at that," he murmured. "We'll see."

Evening came on, cloaking the range with soft shadows. A mocking-bird swooped, dropping its liquid cry on the still air.

"I'm hungry," Red announced.

Robuck chuckled over his solemn earnestness. "You're always hungry," he retorted, making light of the fact that none of them had eaten for hours.

A few minutes later they came upon a tiny creek. Deane drew up, looking at it. "Say," he began; "Red's idea ain't so bad, at that. Come on down to that flat. We'll boil us some coffee."

It required no argument to carry the suggestion. Stepping down on the little brush-surrounded flat they selected, Robuck suddenly froze. At his feet lay the remains of a tiny fire, the ashes not yet beginning to scatter. Red and Jack moved forward as he ran his hand through them.

"Warm yet," he murmured, turning on his knee to shoot a look up at them.

"Brandin' fire?" Red suggested.

"I don't think so," Robuck said slowly. Into his mind flashed remembrance of the bushwhack lead hurled at him the night before. It ran a tautness along his nerves now. "There's somebody not far from here," he added in a low tone, straightening up to glance around toward the brush. "We'd have seen him riding away, if it'd been some cowpoke."

"That's so," Jack conceded. He loosened his gun in the holster. "I never did like lead with my coffee."

"We'll comb the brush," said Robuck.

Before they had fairly begun their search, a gruff hail reached them from up the creek bank. Dusk was thickening now; they saw no more than a vague shape. Their guns came up.

"Easy!" Robuck whipped out the warning. "Come out here where we can see you—and don't make no false moves!"

The other trudged steadily forward, leading his bronc. There was familiarity in his tone as he drew near. "Thought it was you," he said. "I wanted to make sure."

It was Daggett, the Association man.

"You, eh?" Robuck holstered his gun.

Daggett seemed to have forgotten the temper he had displayed at their last meeting. "Yeah," he said easily. "Anythin' goin' on?"

"A bunch of stuff was rustled last night from Mickle's S C spread," Robuck told him. He gave a brief account of the affair, watching Daggett's reaction closely.

Daggett was not surprised. "They've had raids out

there," he nodded. "Reckon this is the first one that didn't come off." Gruff admiration sounded in his voice, not entirely dissembled.

"Daggett," Robuck asked him, "what do you know about Rawlins?"

"Mickle's foreman? . . . He's all right. Leetle on the crusty side, but he means well. Works like hell, I hear."

"What are you doing here?" Robuck flung out abruptly.

Daggett took the switch of subject easily. "This is the only water fer miles around, Robuck. I've seen tracks here before. I purty well know the rustlers water their broncs here. It's a long ways from anywheres; first time I seen the place it set me to thinkin'. I've run myself ragged fer a couple months now—you seen me, way over on the Blackfoot, yoreself. From now on, I'm playin' a waitin' game. If them night-ridin' hombres show up here, you bet yore boots I'll nail 'em!"

"Why tonight?"

"Wal—it'll be a fine night fer their business. Good an' dark—moon up late." Daggett was frank. "I may be wrong, but I'm stickin' here . . . Be glad to have you boys stay for a couple hours," he added.

It was the man's obvious disbelief that they would accept which persuaded Robuck that it was an honest bid for company.

Deane made coffee, and Daggett accepted a cup. They refused his offer of food from the small supply he packed with him.

"You'll need all you've got, if you're staying on here long," Robuck told him.

With the arrival of full night they put out their fire, cached the ponies, and retired to a near-by vantage. Red wanted to go on. "Shucks, there won't be nothin' doin' here," he grumbled. But Robuck said they would stay for a while.

The truth was, he wanted to satisfy himself about Daggett. Either the man was unusually shrewd, or he had nothing to conceal, he decided later. He could detect nothing off-color in the stock detective's answers, nothing cagey in his manner.

Time dragged heavily at this lonely spot. Nothing disturbed the silence. By ten o'clock, even Robuck was wearied with fruitless waiting.

"We'll shove on," he decided.

"Sure," said Daggett. "Mebby there won't be nothin' doin' tonight. But my time'll come. When it does, the fur'll shore fly!"

They left a few minutes later, heading for the Cross 8.

"What you make of him?" Red inquired, in a guarded tone, when they were out of ear-shot.

"Not much," said Robuck. "Why?"

"Queer stock detective, not knowin' a thing about that rustlin'," Red suggested.

"His story seems to hold water," Robuck thought. "He's been keeping to himself. I didn't take to him at first, but maybe I got him wrong . . . It's not a bad idea to watch that water, if you're willing to sit on your tail and wait for things to happen."

"That all?" Red grunted.

Robuck made no reply. The truth was, there remained still in his mind a small reservation as regarded Daggett. Why it was, he could not have told.

The first time they had seen him, Daggett had been following him and Jack. He had given a plausible explanation; had desisted, once he learned their identity. But this second time, again, Robuck could not entirely shake off the feeling that Daggett had been watching them. And this time he had known who they were—else why had he hailed them? Robuck remembered that Daggett had not discovered himself to them until they had begun a search of the creek brush which must eventually have turned him up in any event. Which was it—cleverness, or coincidence?

Unable to make anything of it for the present, he dismissed the matter from his mind.

It was hard on midnight when they drew near the Cross 8. A mile from the ranch, wooded bluffs broke down toward Willow Creek. Threading the trees, they suddenly brought up short at a crashing in the darkness ahead.

"What was that?" Red queried lowly.

"Never mind, what it was!" a sharp voice rang out. "Who are yuh, and what are yuh doin' here?"

They read the unmistakable crackle of warning. The surrounding night was suddenly menacing.

"We're Robuck, Deane and Lefler," Robuck answered promptly; "on our way to the Cross 8. Who are you?"

"Come ahead—slow," the voice responded harshly,

disregarding the last question. "When yuh get to the clearin' in front of yuh, pull up."

Red snorted under his breath. But Robuck was unmoved. "Take it easy," he said. "Do as he says."

They rode forward, stopping in the little opening in the trees. The moon, low as yet, its direct light cut off, cast a diffused glow here.

"All right, boys," muttered the unknown, apparently addressing his hidden companions. "Keep 'em covered, while I make sure of 'em!"

The three saw his dim form detach from the trees. He rode cautiously forward. A dull glint showed at his waist, the leveled six-gun with which he menaced them. He did not pause until he was near enough to stare into Robuck's face. Even then he was dissatisfied.

"Light a match," he snapped.

"Brother," said Robuck, with sudden coolness; "just who are you?"

The other grunted. "Reckon yo're Robuck, all right." He sounded disappointed.

"Why shouldn't I be?" Robuck rapped out. "You're a Cross 8 puncher, aren't you? Why the spooky stuff?"

The other showed a flash of ire. "If you weren't who yuh said yuh were, you'da found out why!" he spat. "Rustlers raided the herd tonight—got away with about thirty head!"

Red swore his amazement, but Robuck was ice. "When did this happen?" he asked swiftly.

"Couple hours ago."

"Anybody see 'em? Was there a fight?"

"Brother, there shore was! Hank Payson's down with a smashed leg—the old man's son was killed."

"Fer Gawd's sake!" Red burst out, unbelievingly. "Young Sam, yuh mean?"

"Sam," the puncher nodded grimly.

"Aw—" Red didn't know how to express himself. He had found much to like in Sam Barron, for all the boy's wildness.

For his part, Robuck's thoughts flashed to Virginia. This would be a heavy blow to her—and to her father, coming on top of his already considerable troubles. An anger such as Robuck had not felt before welled up in him.

"Come on!" he snapped to the others. "We're getting to the ranch!"

They whirled, surged out of the trees and down the bench. "Why in hell'd they have to knock off that kid?" Red was vainly asking himself, as they rode. But Robuck's terse reflections were more to the point. He saw all his suspicions of the day confirmed. The "rustling" on the S C had indeed been a blind, to keep them out of the way while this latest attack on the Cross 8 was being carried out.

"Somebody'll do some explaining, before I'm done with this!" he promised himself.

XII: *Birds of a Feather*

SAM BARRON'S body had been brought to the ranch not long before they arrived there. It proved a stunning blow, leaving Sam's father crushed and directionless, his sister wracked with silent grief.

Punchers, grim and wordless, their jaws clamped and ire flashing in their eyes, hastily saddled up at the corrals. Robuck and his companions, measuring this angry mood, dismounted and quietly entered the house.

Dale Barron looked ten years older. His keen old eyes were lustreless, his shoulders sagged. His voice had lost its boom. It was Red Leffler who stepped to his side in silence, his raw-boned face sympathetic, while Virginia turned to Robuck and Jack.

Side by side they paused, their glances commiserating her. "We heard," Robuck murmured. Tears stood in her eyes, but she was brave; the smile she tried to give them was a wrench to Robuck. Taking a quick step, she gave both her hands to him.

Seeing that instinctive gesture, Deane averted his eye. A flame licked through him, which was not sympathy, but anger and jealousy. Better than words could tell, he knew that the girl was drawn toward Robuck; that such an hour as this clinched her loyalty to him. Face bleak, Jack contemplated the depth to which this barb sank into his stung pride—and found himself standing alone.

He told himself it was rank folly to think such thoughts in this house of tragedy, but it made no difference. Feelings roared through him which it was not in his power to check: Blind rage at circumstance, which had set Robuck before him and over him; increased desire for this girl whose soft, trusting face was even now lifted to the other man. It shook and tossed and had its way with him, making him forget everything save his own loss.

Loss? Deane's jaws hardened, his head came up. This account was not closed yet! Savagely he thrust defeat away from him. It was with quick irritation that he turned to meet an interruption to the powerful sweep of his thoughts.

Trig Borage, Dale Barron's leathery foreman, pulled off his hat as he stepped in. Moving forward awkwardly but firmly, he blurted in an undertone: "We're ready to ride, Dale!"

Catching these significant words, Robuck seemed to come to himself. Giving Virginia an encouraging smile, he released her hands and turned to Trig.

"How many men have you?" he asked.

"Nine," the foreman told him.

Robuck's eyes sought the rancher. "We'll ride with them, Barron," he said. "We'll do everything possible . . . Red, throw our saddles on fresh ponies."

"Broncs are waitin' for yuh, Robuck," Trig thrust in.

"Uh—Robuck'll take charge, Trig," said Dale Barron heavily. "He savvies this game."

Borage nodded.

Without more words, they walked out. The Cross 8 crew waited in the yard. Swinging up, Robuck's backward glance fell on Virginia, standing in the door. She had eyes only for him. Her look pleaded with him to be careful. A moment later, Robuck and Borage in the lead, the cavalcade rode into the night.

The foreman gave a concise account of the disastrous raid as they made for that part of the range where it had taken place. The rustlers, nearly a dozen strong, had swept boldly out of the timber, to cut out a bunch of grazing steers under the astonished eyes of the night hawk. His warning shots had brought three other riders, one of them Sam Barron, to the spot on the run. Outnumbered as they were, the four had jumped the rustlers, with the inevitable result. Fighting off pursuit, the rustlers had disappeared into the southwest.

With the aid of the moon, the posse picked up the trail without difficulty. It led off into the ragged border of the Blackfoot desert. The steers had been hazed along at top speed.

Robuck found himself unable to keep his thoughts from looping away from his immediate concerns. The day's events built themselves up in a clearly readable pattern: He was now certain that the affair which had taken them out to the S C had been deliberately planned. Daggett came in for his share of examination. Robuck asked himself whether the man had not been determined to delay them, with his story of watching the isolated creek. But for him, they would have been on the Cross 8 at the time of the raid.

Whatever Daggett's actual status, it was plain that he, like Rawlins, would stand close watching.

Deane's thoughts were likewise busy. He faced none of the bewildering uncertainties which confronted Robuck. To him all this was clear reading. Spokey Withers, Rawlins, Daggett—these three, and probably others, were strong links in the chain binding Dunc Mickle to the lawlessness which clutched the Flathead range by the throat. Remembering the last conference with the banker, Deane penetrated the stratagem behind the occurrences of the day as easily as if he had overheard its planning.

What Virginia Barron had said concerning her father's troubles was the clue to Mickle's secret activities. Dreams of empire plagued Dunc. Reckless of consequences, he was using Smoke Devlin's wild bunch to further his ends. Tonight's raid was a part of the plan to break Dale Barron, drive him out. Barron's ruin would remove from Mickle's path the only considerable obstacle on this side of Flathead.

Conning it in its entirety, Deane perceived the diabolical cleverness of the scheme. "It's air-tight," he approved. "But not so tight that I can't do something about it myself," he mused, smiling grimly as he found his own account in the tangle of motives involved.

For the first time, he began to entertain a tangible hope of winning Virginia. He had seen strong combinations before; knew this machine of Dunc Mickle's to be such a one. Moreover, it suited his needs exactly. From now on, he resolved, as detectives, he, Robuck and Red Leffler, would signally fail. Time and ridicule would drive Robuck out of the country. Deane himself would throw in with this local crowd; have money. With the downfall of her father, Virginia would have no home, no one to turn to. Once Robuck was out of the picture, Jack had no doubt of his ability to draw the girl to him and hold her. She would be grateful to him, and soften. . . .

Where this was taking him with his partners, he thoroughly understood. He did not care. He was on his own now. So firmly was he set on his course that when Robuck asked him, with customary crispness, to cover the outside of the rustlers' trail in the brush, Jack chose to refuse.

"Do it yourself," he replied calmly, but with unmistakable intent.

Robuck glanced at him sharply. This was not the Deane he knew. "No time to kick over the traces, Jack," he reprimanded quietly. "We've got to work together on this."

It startled him, as he ceased, to realize that this was the first time he had ever spoken thus to the other. But if Deane noticed it, he gave no sign, wrapped in his own thoughts. Robuck directed a puncher to do what he had asked, and the matter was dropped.

Toward dawn, the trail of the rustlers entered a flinty stretch of country, barren of growth. In half-an-hour they lost the sign they had been following. Ahead and on either side, lava beds stretched away, endless and enigmatic.

After a methodical hunt, Trig Borage was ready to admit defeat. It was another hour before Robuck gave up. At last he waved the posse together.

"We'll call it a day," he told them. "They got away from us."

He failed to note the quizzical smile on Deane's face as they turned back toward the Cross 8, his thoughts busy with the difficult task of telling Dale Barron the disappointing results of their pursuit. While this night's work only strengthened his determination to solve the stubborn case, he knew that for the time being, it would plunge the rancher deeper than ever into discouragement.

Hours later, when the three had returned to Flathead, Dunc Mickle listened in silence to their report of events. He shook his head and clucked sympathetically over Barron's loss, and the blow dealt him by the death of his son. Over the reclaiming of his own S C steers he nodded grudingly, but gave the unmistakable impression that the detectives could hardly be said to be giving satisfaction.

"I'll put matters up to the Association in the best light I can manage," he said with the air of a concession, pursing his lips; "but I don't know how they'll feel about this." He simulated a masterly reluctance. "I'm afraid you'll have to do better, or look for somethin' else to do. And remember my advice, now—"

"Mickle, how long has Rawlins worked for you?" Robuck asked abruptly.

Dunc's glance sharpened. "Six years," he said shortly. "Why?"

"Do you trust him?"

All Mickle's authority seemed to flow into his manner. "What are you drivin' at, Robuck?" he demanded.

"I asked you a simple question," Robuck told him easily.

"And the answer is yes!"

Robuck nodded. To Dunc's boring inquiries he replied blandly that he had said all he had to say. Mickle scowled, became testy. Jack, reading between the lines, was more sure than ever of his ground.

After supper, taking leave of his companions at the hotel, Deane walked down past the bank. A light burned there. Mickle, it appeared, was in the habit of spending the evenings at his desk.

Deane thought he understood the advantage Dunc found in following the custom, and he was not disappointed. Before nine o'clock he saw Spokey Withers jog into town, rack his pony at the Ox-Yoke and saunter down the street. In front of the bank Spokey loitered for some minutes, finishing a smoke; then abruptly disappeared in an alley siding the bank. Deane knew that in a moment Dunc Mickle would be letting the little man into the bank by the rear door.

He would have given much to overhear that conference, but perhaps there was little he could not glean from a rough guess. Entering the alley Spokey had used, he located the bank's rear entrance, then seated himself on a box a dozen feet away. Here he waited.

At ten o'clock the door rattled, jarred open. Spokey

stepped out, Dunc Mickle with him. After a last, murmuring exchange, Spokey started down the alley.

"Mind you tell him what I say, and that I mean business!" was Dunc's guarded conclusion.

"He won't forget," Deane murmured across the gloom, as Spokey's form faded from sight. "I'll stake a lot on that."

Mickle started visibly. After the light of the bank, this alley had seemed pitch-dark to him and Spokey; neither had observed Deane, silent and motionless on his box. Now Dunc probed the shadows with craggy sharpness. Jack saved him trouble by moving easily into the glow from the door. The banker raked his impassive face for a moment with wordless suspicion.

His words came with chilling harshness: "What do you want around here?"

"I want to talk to you," Deane told him composedly.

Mickle's eyes were like diamond points. He jerked a grudging nod. "This is no time for it," he grunted. "But come inside."

He turned into the building, and Deane, fully assured, followed.

"Now," Dunc began, with an assumption of briskness, seating himself at his desk. "What is it that you've got to say?"

He did not ask Deane to sit down, but Jack, entirely at ease, availed himself of the vacant chair standing beside the desk.

"I see Withers paid you a little visit," he remarked, with apparent irrelevance.

"What of that?" Mickle barked impatiently.

"Nothing," Jack responded; "except this: The last time I had word of Spokey Withers' movements, he was seen riding away from Smoke Devlin's hideout, Mickle." He met the other's gaze squarely.

Dunc half-rose from his seat, indignation mounting in his bony visage. Whatever his impulse, however, he thought better of it, sinking back.

"I don't understand what you're drivin' at, Deane!" he got out.

"Yes, you do," Jack told him grimly. "But this is it: I know you've got dealin's with Smoke Devlin."

Mickle stiffened, exploding: "Poppycock! Whoever heard of such twaddle? . . . If there's nothin' but this foolishness on your mind, I'll have to ask you—"

"No," Jack contradicted coolly. "You won't ask me to go, Mickle. And I'll tell you why—I know too much."

The rich claret in Mickle's cheeks receded slightly. His gaze fixed. Plainly holding himself in bitter check, he spoke with difficulty.

"Suppose you tell me what it is," he said with dangerous softness; "since you know so much."

Deane hardened suddenly, leaning forward and speaking flat words. "I'll tell you a few things, Mickle, that'll cool you off: You want to grab the Barron ranch. You're tied up with Smoke Devlin to help you out; Spokey Withers is your go-between. You hired us, when you learned we were going to stick around anyway, to keep a finger on us. You were mad because we nailed a couple of men at Salt Fork!" He began to talk faster, more compellingly, as Mickle, apoplectic, attempted to head him off. "Yesterday, Mickle, you sent us off on a wild goose chase—warned us to stick together—set your man Daggett to watching us! Have I got anything on you? Why, you're in this to your eyebrows!" Se sat back, a cynical smile on his lips, and waited for Mickle to speak.

Dunc had gone gray, boring him with winkless, obsidian eyes, as the indictment ran on to its relentless and damning end. He sat motionless for a moment, hatred and leaping fear tugging at his flattened lips.

"A pretty story!" he attempted to sneer, as though recovering from stupefying surprise. "If you think you can prove such a preposterous, libelous farrago—"

"Let that go," Deane directed, with a mirthless grin. "You can be sure that if I decide to, I'll come damn near to provin' it!"

"What do you expect me to do?" Dunc flared helplessly.

Jack laid a finger on the desk, meeting his gaze narrowly. "You'll either take care of me," he stipulated, in a smooth, silky voice; "or take the consequences!"

Dunc choked. His visage darkened; a vein throbbed in his forehead. "Man, this is blackmail!" he protested thickly.

"What do you call what you're tryin' to do to Dale Barron and some others?" Deane inquired shrewdly.

Mickle began to sweat. "You're mad!" he cried. He sat thinking desperately. "But I can't afford a scandal. What would you consider . . ." He paused.

"A fair price for keepin' my mouth shut?" Jack interposed coolly. 'Well, we'll say twenty thousand dollars."

Horrified at his effrontery, Mickle felt the naked steel of panic bite into his soul. He knew better than to show it, uttering a bark of sardonic laughter.

"Tight-fisted old curmudgeon!" Deane was inwardly thinking. He felt sure he had Mickle at his mercy, but something warned him against overplaying his hand. He said: "That figure don't suit you? Suppose you name your own. I'll decide whether I like it."

Dunc was swift to grasp this advantage. He pressed it even further. "Deane, you're a detective," he pointed out shrewdly. "How do I know you wouldn't gouge me and forget it?"

Jack grinned dryly. "You don't know it," he retorted brazenly.

Mickle shook his head. "We can't do business," he said decisively. "I told you you've got me all wrong. I'd rather fight you, than—"

"What do you want from me?" Jack snapped.

Craftiness got into Mickle's mien. "If you was to see to it that Robuck and this Leffler got out of the country, I might make it worth your while," he suggested cautiously.

"Give me your figure!" Jack directed brusquely.

"Well, I'm hard-up right now—"

"I don't give a damn about that!" Deane ground out. "Either you talk my language, or, Mickle, you'll never lay hands on the Barron spread!" He added: "It'll be ten thousand dollars. Take it or leave it!"

Dunc simulated dismay. "Ten thousand!" he jerked

out. "Why, I can't—" He paused, speculated wildly. "All—all right," he capitulated grudgingly. "We'll put it like this, Deane—five thousand now, and five thousand when Robuck and that other one are gone."

Jack gauged him sharply. At length he gave a curt nod. "It's a deal," he said.

Mickle floundered to his feet. Without another word he entered the vault. One of the safes there was not of the time-lock variety; Dunc manipulated its dial for a moment, then threw it open. When he shut it and returned, it was to hand over five thousand dollars in bills of odd denominations.

Deane nodded, counting it and stuffing it away. "I'll keep my bargain, Mickle," he grunted; "and you keep the other five thousand ready . . . Any dry-gulcher you put on my trail in the meantime," he concluded with thin warning, "will be extra."

Dunc shot him a single blistering look of baffled hatred as he turned out into the night.

XIII: *The Last Trail*

FOR two days Robuck put forth his best efforts to find some trace of the raiders who had left Sam Barron dead on the range. He turned up nothing, nor did he learn in what direction the rustled stock had been driven out of the country.

He, Red and Deane attended Sam's funeral. Afterward, ranchers from all over the Flathead range wanted to discuss events. Listening attentively, Robuck heard nothing to his advantage.

On the following day he rode by himself to the lonely creek at which they had left Daggett on guard. There were a few questions which he desired to put to the man. But Daggett was gone. No tracks he found there were less than a day old. Whether Daggett himself had pulled out on the night of the raid on the Cross 8, could not be determined.

Robuck rode back to Flathead to receive from Red the news that Broke Horan, the cattle buyer, had been seen. Horan, the story went, had ridden boldly into town. On hearing the Association detectives were there, however, he had done a quick fade. Red declared the man was still in hiding somewhere on the poorer side of town; but Deane, who reconnoitered the neighborhood with Red, scouted the idea that Horan was in Flathead or had even been there.

"Somebody else was mistaken for him," was Jack's verdict. "Horan wouldn't be fool enough to show up here."

Wade Shandler knew nothing about the matter. After a vain attempt to locate the man reported to have seen Horan, Robuck turned his mind to other concerns. He had not yet forgotten the train robbery which had determined him to bring Smoke Devlin and his long-riders to book. Recalling how those men had circulated freely in Flathead before the hold-up, he asked himself whether there was not yet someone in town who might lead him to the outlaw's present headquarters.

Red, however, was not satisfied. Through the afternoon and into the evening he prowled the tumbledown precincts which he suspected of harboring Horan. One spot in particular interested him—the stable at which Smoke Devlin's crowd had waited on the night of the express-car robbery. Without showing his interest, Red watched the place for a long time. He saw nothing of Broke Horan; but toward ten o'clock a man came out of the weathered house to stand on the porch. Later he stepped into the street, to meet, as if by accident, a stroller whose high and blocky shape could be that of none other than Jack Deane. And the man he spoke to was Spokey Withers!

After a few guarded words the two moved off into the shadows, where they murmured for some time. Red was unable to get close enough to overhear them. The fact only succeeded in exciting his keenest interest. What, he asked himself, could be the meaning of such a meeting?

He didn't know. But later, following Deane down street to the Ox-Yoke, and entering the place a few minutes after the other, for the space of an hour he hung on Jack's lightest word. Robuck was there. They talked of a number of things; but not once did Deane refer to any conversation with Withers.

His suspicions awakening, Red later found occasion to speak to Jack alone. "I see you bumped into this Spokey Withers tonight," he said off-handedly, watching Deane's face narrowly. "What'd he have to say fer himself?"

Deane displayed no surprise. His response was almost idle. "Saw us, did you? . . . Thought maybe I could get something out of him about Horan. He don't know I know he's hooked up with Devlin."

In spite of himself, Red bristled. "Well, Withers was there himself! Why didn't yuh grab him?"

Jack smiled. "What good would that do, when you're after bigger fish?" he countered, so reasonably that Red felt at a loss.

"Get anythin' outa Spokey?"

"No, he's pretty close-mouthed."

"Why didn't yuh tell Bill about it?" Red demanded.

Deane shrugged. "Why should I? There was nothing to tell."

He carried it off so well that Red let the matter drop, with reservations concerning the soundness of his partner's judgment. The time was coming when he was to hark back to the incident with even shrewder suspicion; when it occurred to him, indeed, that there had been something furtive and clandestine about that meeting which Jack had neglected to mention.

In the meantime, they were thrown into fresh activities which kept them all busy. On the following morning, a Cross 8 puncher sought out Robuck with word that Dale Barron wanted to see him at once. Robuck, scenting some new lead, readily assented.

Riding out to the ranch, he found Barron almost belligerent. The latter took him aside without delay, and growled resentfully: "Robuck, I got wind of a raid that's goin' to be pulled on my spread tonight!" Bristling with indignation, he gave the details of how he had come by the tip.

Robuck listened to the end, then asked: "Who else knows about this?"

"Wal—some of the boys who was out here to the funeral: Ike Greer, Stacey McCall, Cal McDonough." They were all ranchers, old friends of Barron. "They're willin' to throw in an' help block this raid—reckon they're gettin' plumb worried about the rustlin'," the rancher explained.

Robuck nodded. "I'll be here with my boys. We'll throw a guard around the range. Maybe we can nab these gents."

It did not occur to him to doubt the validity of Barron's information. His previous leads he recognized as having come, in each instance, from a doubtful source; but there could be no question of the Cross 8 owner's honesty, and the sincerity of his desire to put a stop to the depredations.

Careful plans were laid for the night's activities.

With a posse of ranchers ready to hand, and stinging under Dunc Mickle's bland criticisms, on his return to town Robuck determined to say nothing concerning the expected raid. He simply told Deane and Red that they would ride out to the Cross 8 that afternoon. Arriving there late, they found nearly a score of waiting range men, all heavily armed; all grimly prepared for anything.

Dale Barron told them that Robuck was in charge, and they accepted him without question. He immediately put his plan into effect, stationing men at intervals in a great circle enclosing the Cross 8 range. No time was lost, yet it was nearing dark when Deane, Lefler and several punchers rode south to take up their positions in low hills bordering the Blackfoot wastes.

Deane was in command here, in Robuck's absence. He disposed his men across several shallow range hollows, and was telling Red that he expected him to guard a rocky defile half-a-mile away, when the sorrel-headed one exploded with his usual frankness.

"A swell general, you are!" he snorted. "Yuh got every crack and hole in the wall plugged—except this nice wide hollow right here! Or don'tcha reckon rustlers ride where the goin's easy?"

"Never mind," Jack told him impatiently. "I'll be here, myself. Doesn't that suit you?"

"Not very damn well!" Red fired back. "What yuh gonna do alone, if a dozen of them birds ride in here and jump yuh all of a sudden?"

Deane was grim. "You turn your bronc and go where you're told to go!" he snapped harshly.

Red was used to having almost anything said to him in fun. But now his jaw dropped. "Jack," he began soberly; "if yuh wasn't a friend of mine—"

"Were you put in charge here, or was I?" Jack cut him off abruptly, with cold ferocity.

Red stared at him for a moment, his bony face reddening. Then turning his pony, he jogged away, muttering to himself.

Full dark stole over the range. The brush songsters twittered sleepily and fell silent. A hush like the slumber of the world descended on these timeless hills. And there was something else in the night—an unseen menace closing in on all sides, tightening men's nerves and leaving them sharply expectant.

At eleven o'clock the echoes awakened to the flat crack of spaced shots. Around the far-flung guard circle, men snapped to alertness. There could be no mistaking that thin, insistent summons! Within a few moments, riders were converging from every direction on the point from which those shots had sounded.

Robuck, his bronc reined in, was trying to place the spot in his mind's eye. It was off in Deane's territory, he decided; and yet deeper into the range than that. Did it mean that the raiders had broken through the cordon at some point? Without awaiting an answer, he rammed home the spurs, went storming through the brush.

More shots, a savage burst, ripped the night. They were nearer now. Topping a swell, Robuck saw pencilled daggers of flame, heard the sharp pound of roofs. A harsh yell rang out. Then, vaguely, he made out the band of steers rushing madly south, hazed along by high, dark shapes from which the defiant flashes of gunfire came.

The story was plain. The rustlers had slipped through, snapped up a bunch of Cross 8 stock, and started away—without the slightest warning until this eleventh hour. Robuck knew a moment's stinging anger that his stern orders should have been somewhere ignored. Then he was plunging toward the head of that shadowy drive.

A dusky shape swept up beside him. Robuck flung a stabbing look across. "Red? . . . We've got to ride those gents down!" he jerked out lowly. "The circle must be broken—they know where they're heading for!"

Red growled some reply. Suddenly, flinging up his gun, he blazed away at the raiders. Their challenging, warning yells whipped back. Swift lances of fire freckled the darkness.

Robuck's jaws clamped as his bronc faltered. It regained its stride. Bitter determination seared through him, made him fire and ice. In the doings of this night he smelled treachery and worse. Had his associates glimpsed his face in this moment they would scarcely have recognized him.

Try as he would, he could draw up no more on the thundering raiders. They curved sharply away from him and Red; they had to ply their spurs unmercifully to hold their ground, but they did it. Robuck was using his gun now, deliberately trying to target those darting forms, briefly flitting, as swiftly gone. The rumble of hoofs and the fear-crazed bellowing of steers was a tumult, over which the crack of weapons lay thin and flat and ominous. The yells of infuriated ranchers and cowboys, closing in from every direction, made a savage background of sound. Death was riding this range tonight.

It was Red who, pressing fearlessly close, first discovered that the raiders had abandoned their steers. He let out a bull roar. Guns flashed at him with snarling fury; Robuck saw him sag on his racing pony. But he was only crouching. An instant later he replied fiercely, charging the rustlers as though he would run them down. Somehow they kept ahead.

So swiftly had the fight moved that Robuck's entire force, closing in on the point from which it had started, were swept to the rear before they became aware of what was happening. Ahead of the raiders lay nothing more menacing than the open range; and they seemed aware of it. At a gruff order from one of their number, they started to split up, facing backward and lashing out with a lethal hail of lead, no longer fearful of cutting down their own kind.

Chagrin cleft Robuck's hard thinking at that maneuver. He knew suddenly that some of the rustlers would certainly escape, perhaps all of them—but he hung on doggedly, even when he found himself hounding a single fugitive. As if he understood where his salvation lay, this man struck for a rocky ridge carved with gullies, and ceased firing. His bronc was fleet as the wind. A few minutes later, only an occasional hoof-crack drifted back. At the shoulder of the granite ridge he disappeared. Nor was he to be picked up again.

Robuck cursed once, and, savage disappointment in his heart, swung back. He began to meet other pursuers, as luckless as himself. It was half-an-hour before, finally gathering, they learned the extent of their failure. The Cross 8 steers had been saved, but Cal McDonough had a slug in the groin picked up early in the fight; several others had grazes; a crippled pony had to be shot. The rustlers had escaped to a man.

"Wal, they done it again," Dale Barron growled, unsuccessfully attempting to dissemble his regret. "We might's well figure to get us some shut-eye."

"Not a bit of it," Robuck thrust in decisively. He had not forgotten the train robbery during which only the audacity of the outlaws had turned failure into success. "We blocked a raid, all right; but those hombres are still in circulation. We're stickin' right here!"

There was discussion of the necessity for this. Finally, Robuck's suggestion carried, the men broke up to return to their original positions. Red Lefler, busy with his own thoughts, rode beside Jack Deane in silence.

"Dang foolishness!" Deane muttered disgustedly. "There's no use of us millin' around here till daylight, now it's all over."

"You should talk!" Red burst out furiously. "Dammit all, if it wasn't fer you, this never would've happened this way!"

Jack reined in with a jerk. "What are you drivin' at?" he grunted menacingly.

"You know what I'm gettin' at!" Red charged. "Them birds got through on our side, there ain't no two ways about it—and it was on account of the way yuh spread us out!"

"Red—!" Deane began, with mounting ire. "Don't you go too far with me!"

Instead of exploding, Red spoke gravely, out of the depths of real responsibility. "I don't know what's come over yuh, Jack. Yo're different 'n yuh used to be. When Robuck said he couldn't savvy how come them skunks sneaked through us, did yuh speak up and say mebby it was yore fault? Yuh did not! . . . I ain't forgot that little talk of yores with Spokey Withers, neither," he added thinly.

"And so what?" Deane snapped.

"Jack, it looks mighty like you was givin' us the double-cross," said Red steadily.

"Damn your loose tongue!" Deane, suddenly in a black rage, jammed his pony over against Red's. Stirrup to stirrup, they stared into each other's eyes; and it was Deane who finally gave way, shrugging himself together with a mutter which sounded like "What's the use?"

"You think it over, brother: that's all I got to say!" Red threw into him. "When Bill begins to put two and two together, yuh better have yore answers ready!"

"Drop it, can't you?" Jack jerked out exasperatedly.

"When you do, I will," retorted Red significantly.

They rode on, reached the hollow where Deane had stood guard alone. This time, Red chose to stay there also, drifting or remaining still for long intervals, but keeping a pointed distance of fifty yards or more between them.

Apprehensions gnawed at Deane. "What does he know? Has he really got a line on me?" he asked himself. Baffled anger roared through him, his face hardening to stone. He had no intention of letting Lefler stand between him and the scheme he had worked out.

He pictured Red dogging him, building upon his suspicions. Desperation quickened his already taut muscles.

"I've got to do something!" he whispered tensely. "I can't shoot the man . . . Can I?"

On the heels of this burning thought, so closely that it might have been an answer, the hollow, echoing spang of a rifle rang out. Deane didn't see the muzzle light. But he heard the sickening dull smack of the striking lead, over in Red's direction. He heard Red's wrenching groan. He saw the paralyzed shape cant over and slide out of the saddle.

"God!"

So closely had action approximated his unspoken, groping wish that Deane was rocked to the depths. Sweat started out on his body. Frozen in his position, he did not at once go to Red, probing the menacing night wildly until he got a grip on himself. When he broke from his trance, men came pounding out of the darkness, drawn by the breaking echoes of the shot. They found him dismounting beside his prostrate partner.

"Who is that? . . . What happened, anyhow?" the quick queries came.

Deane found himself in an ironic situation, the significance of which the others did not grasp; must never be allowed to grasp. He made no immediate response, but he received a shock when Robuck pushed through the others abruptly, coming to his side.

"Who is it?" Robuck rapped out. Stooping to peer, he gave a violent jerk. "Good Lord! It's Red! . . . Is he hard hit?"

"I don't—know."

They ascertained quickly that the rifle slug had struck near the heart, and that Red was breathing his last. He was unconscious. Springing to his feet, Robuck got out in a strangled voice: "How did this happen?"

Without revealing his previous exchange with Red, Deane told exactly what had occurred. Robuck broke in at the end, fiercely:

"Who was on the range, who could have wanted him dead? Did we have one of the rustlers trapped here, without knowing it?"

It was incredible, save in the case of a man unable to travel. This part of the range had been deserted during the running fight. Without instructions, men began to circle the locality. They met no one, drifted back.

Red gasped out his life in Robuck's arms.

Dawn fingers were lifting the lid of darkness when the ranchers began quietly to drift away to their homes. Red was removed to the Cross 8. After a silent breakfast, Robuck directed Deane to carry their dead partner in to Flathead, to be shipped East to a brother in Iowa. Himself, Robuck remained behind, oblivious of Dale Barron's gruff words or the pitying glances of Virginia. He was stunned; he wanted to be alone. Moreover, he wanted to examine the scene of Red's murder.

Riding to town, Deane was having a rough time of it. He would have given anything in his power to be far removed from the accusative corpse of his erstwhile partner. Instead, he was its sole companion. Shuddering, he tried again and again to persuade himself he had had nothing to do with this murder. He *had* not; and yet, those damning thoughts of his which had led up to it. . . .

It was a vast relief when Flathead hove in view. Riding in hurriedly, he lost no time in arranging with the undertaker, a wagon-maker who constructed coffins, and the baggage man at the station, for the disposal of Red. That done, he retired at length to the Ox-Yoke. He drank heavily, feeling that he needed it. Robuck had given him no further instructions, nor did he put in an appearance. Evening found Deane walking the street, endeavoring to collect his scattered thoughts. It was early when he turned toward his room.

Shortly after dark a soft knock came at his door. Jack unconsciously started. Scowling, he turned to the door, flung it open as though he had nothing to conceal. He was astonished when Dunc Mickle slipped in and hastily closed the door behind him. There was an ironic smile on Mickle's face; but Jack's frown became thunderous.

"Shandler told me all about it," Dunc began lowly,

rubbing his hands. "It was a surprise to me, but it couldn't have turned out better!"

"What are you coming here for?" Deane interrupted peremptorily. "Damn it all, Mickle; my room is no place to—"

"Keep your voice down!" Dunc reprimanded him sharply.

Jack's furious words were a murmur: "You know what it means to us if we're caught meeting in corners, you fool! If you can't use better sense, I don't want anything to do with you!"

Mickle's smile became sardonic. "Talk, Deane!" he scoffed. "Just talk! There's no need of us to bluff each other. Remember that." He plunged into a discussion of the raid on the Cross 8. Jack grudgingly supplied him with the facts.

Mickle nodded sagely at the end. "That's one of 'em out of the way," he said easily, with thin meaning. "If an accident happens to Robuck, I won't make any complaint, either."

Deane's scalp lifted with something like horror as he heard himself coolly credited with a murder he had not committed. Mickle took it for granted that he had shot down his partner in cold blood. It made his veins run cold.

"Mickle," he ground out; "if you think I—"

"Where's Robuck now?" Dunc broke in blandly. "Did you say he stayed out at Barron's spread?"

Deane stared at him with burning eyes for a tense moment, then relaxed, swallowing with difficulty. He nodded. "He's out there," he muttered thickly.

"Having a look around, likely," Mickle nodded. His hard eyes glinting with some thought of his own, he quickly changed the subject for the few remaining moments before he slipped out. "Don't forget—" were his last, jarring words; "that other five thousand is waitin' for you, Deane."

Sinking on the bed, Deane gazed vacantly at the closed door for a long time.

XIV: *Wolf Sign*

ROBUCK rode away from the ranch glad for just one thing: that he was a detective. That Red Lefler—big, genial, homely, raw-boned Red—was no more, seemed impossible to believe. Yet it was true enough. His eyes cold, for this hour Robuck forgot the rustling and the robbery he had sworn to square. There was no room for them in his numbed brain. He meant to avenge Red's murder if he never did anything else.

It was no task to find again the place where Red had been shot. The skyline of the hollow was printed in Robuck's brain in lineaments of fire.

Nothing near the blood-stained spot where his partner had expired in his arms gave him any lead. Remounting, he began to circle away, wider and wider. Behind a low outcrop of rock on the gentle slope a hundred yards away he found what he sought. Here in the dust were the marks, from toes to elbows, where a man had lain outstretched. More than that, the imprint of a rifle-stock was plain. Robuck nodded, his long lips drawn thin. Here the killer had hidden.

Heel-prints led up the slope to a point where a pony had been tethered in tall brush for perhaps an hour. Robuck followed its departing tracks for a few yards, saw that they were plain, and turned back. At the place where the assassin had laid, he dismounted and began to search thoroughly. At length he was rewarded. A little apart, almost hidden in a rocky crevice where the ejector had thrown it, he found an empty cartridge case.

A 30-30 of a popular make, it told him nothing. Jack Deane packed a rifle which shot such cartridges. He did himself. So he drew no special information from this find. Yet he was moving steadily toward certain conclusions concerning this murder which puzzled him.

Remounting, he set out to follow the trail of the killer's bronc. It led south half-a-mile through masking brush, after which it took to better going. Several miles farther on, the murderer had struck into a cattle trail leading to creek water. Here the pony tracks faded out, covered by drifting steers. Robuck persevered, quartering and cutting ahead until he had covered every conceivable avenue of escape. But the assassin's tracks eluded him.

He turned back, his thoughts busy. The single certainty he possessed concerning the killer confounded him.

"It wasn't one of the raiders," he soliloquized. "The man who did this job was riding a lone trail. Now, who . . ."

The start he gave was telegraphed to his pony. The animal stopped, turning its head inquiringly; but Robuck was unaware, his mind racing. Who did he know who was riding the range alone—who he had reason to believe had been watching him and his partners? The name leaped at him—Daggett!

Late in the morning, he drew rein before the bank in

Flathead, dismounted and strode in. Mickle was talking with some merchant at his desk. He was soon free.

"Mickle," Robuck began without preliminaries, "how good an idea have you where your man Daggett keeps himself?"

A cool warning brushed Dunc's nerves. He preserved his calm briskness. "I know where he is all the time, Robuck. Why?"

"I want to know exactly where he was last night."

"He was on my X L range, seventy miles west," said Mickle promptly. "I happen to know that for a fact." His glance focused to sharpness. "If you're tinkering with the idea that he had anything to do with the lamentable death of your partner, get it out of your head. There's nothing to it!"

The blank wall against which Robuck's every lead turned him, left him curt. He did not particularly disbelieve Mickle, but he thought the man might himself be deceived. He decided to look over the hitch-racks for an X L bronc, single out its rider, and put a few questions. He was still occupied with this when he ran into Jack Deane at noon.

"Red taken care of?" he queried.

Deane nodded. "Better stop in the undertaker's if you want to see him. He's goin' east tonight on twenty-eight."

The extent of his loss swept Robuck afresh. It left his face bleak, as he described his morning's activities.

Jack nodded sympathetically. "Shall we ride out to the Cross 8 this afternoon?" he queried, at the end of the discussion.

Robuck's negative was flat. "I'm hunting for a lead," he pointed out. The glance he flicked at the other was one of disfavor. "You don't seem to be much bothered by the fact that our pal's been killed, Jack."

"Sure, it means plenty to me!" Deane protested quickly. "But what can we do?"

"We can try to do something," was Robuck's rebuking response. "This evening'll be plenty of time to go out to the Cross 8."

"You going out then?"

"Yes."

A moment later, filled with his driving concerns, Robuck turned away. Deane stood looking after, busy with his own thoughts. Presently he walked down to Kemmer's stable and took up his stand in the big doorway. The place was deserted. He was there alone when Dunc Mickle came along, on his way back to the bank after dinner.

"I want a word with you," Jack murmured.

The faint frown on Dunc's severe face was habitual. He glanced quickly along the street, and stepped in the stable. A moment later they faced each other in the dusky, strong-smelling office.

"What is it?" the banker clipped off.

Confident of the potency of what he had to say, Deane spoke deliberately. "Mickle, can you get hold of Spokey this afternoon?"

"Yes?"

Jack's murmur was freighted: "Tell him to get word to Devlin that Robuck will be out at Barron's Granite Basin line-camp sometime tonight—"

"What!" Mickle exclaimed, startled.

"—And that whatever happens to Robuck," Jack finished levelly, "will be between him and Smoke."

Dunc stared. "Barron don't use the Basin after June," he objected. "It's burnt dry. Are you sure Robuck'll be there?"

Jack assented grimly. "That camp will be deserted. That's why I name it."

Mickle was full of questions, but Deane cut him off. "You don't know a thing about this," he reminded; "and you don't need to. There's just one thing more I want from you—a messenger you can trust. Do you know such a man?"

Mickle hesitated. "Where does he go?"

"He takes a note out to the Cross 8."

Dunc thought it over, something sinister coming into his black eyes. He nodded, believing he saw it all. "I can fix it up. When do you want him?"

"Tell him to meet me in the dry creek bed a mile south of town, at five o'clock."

A few moments later they parted. Deane repaired to his room at the hotel, where he spent an hour composing his note. That finished, he returned to the street. The afternoon seemed interminable. At length, however, the shadows began to run out. Stopping in at a hash-house for an early bite, and making sure that Robuck was not about, Deane saddled up and rode out of town. Circling wide, he came finally to the dry creek bed, and there, concealed from chance range riders, he waited.

The minutes dragged, and he found himself on edge.

He gave a start when, with a clatter of pebbles, a lean, ferret-faced man of forty-five turned his bronc down into the old stream course and jogged forward.

"You waitin' fer me?" said this individual colorlessly.

"Mickle sent you? . . . All right. We'll push off for the Cross 8."

The man hesitated. "You goin' too? What yuh want me fer, then?"

"Leave that to me!" Jack snapped testily. "I'm not going all the way."

They turned out of the old bed and set off, riding easily. Deane said they had plenty of time. The lowering sun touched the serrated horizon in the west and the sky warmed to sunset colors. They had not followed the wagon road to the Cross 8, striking across the open range. Three or four miles from the ranch, Deane drew up in a fringe of trees.

"You go on alone from here," he said. "Take this note to Virginia Barron; see that she gets it herself." He handed it over. "And say as little as possible. If there's any talk at all, you've just come from Granite Basin line-camp, do you savvy? And you're on your way to town for a doctor for a wounded man—in a hurry. As soon as you can, get away from there. But find out what she's going to do. Got all that?"

The messenger's assent was noncommittal. "Yuh wanta see me again, I take it?"

"Yes. Follow the ranch road toward town. After a couple of miles you pass a wooded ridge on your right. I'll be waiting there."

The man nodded, but did not offer to make an immediate start, fumbling with his cinches. Deane watched him for a moment, then jerked out: "Did Mickle pay you, or didn't he?"

"He didn't pay me fer nothin'."

Scowling, Jack dug out a ten dollar bill. "Plaster that across your mouth," he grunted.

Tucking the money away, the man dug in his spurs and shot down the ridge. When he was gone from sight, Deane turned his bronc and rode slowly west in the direction of the rendezvous.

Sunset was a blaze of glory now, smeared across the western sky. He was unaware of it, save as it affected visibility. Already the wooded patches were dusky; between the ridges, pooled shadows thickened. Crossing such a hollow, he suddenly paused to sweep his backtrail with a careful glance. There was nothing. Attributing his eerie feeling to the uncertainty of this night's plans, he rode on.

Crossing the trail to the Barron ranch, he again experienced the sharp suspicion that scrutinizing eyes were following him. He abandoned his intention of waiting in the open, turning into the trees edging the ridge on which he had told his messenger he would wait.

The glow in the west began to fade. Already the eastern sky was darkening, the first stars visible. Deane half-pulled his tobacco sack from his pocket, jammed it back impatiently. "It's takin' that bird a hell of a long time to get there and back!" he muttered.

Just before dusk thickened, he heard a horse coming

down the trail from the ranch. Taking no chances, he drew back into thicker cover. The on-coming pony swung off the trail, drifted this way. An alert scrutiny from behind a tree satisfied him that its rider was the man whom he waited. He pushed forward.

"Was she there? What did she say?" the queries spilled out of him with unusual fluency. He hung on the reply.

The messenger nodded. "Yeah, I give 'er the note. It shore spooked her up. She didn't hardly see me at all."

"What did she do?" Deane demanded.

"Wal, she milled around some, and finally lined out fer the corrals. The' wasn't much of anybody around. I reckon she's takin' out right prompt."

It was all that Jack had waited to learn. He began to jump his pony away, then turned back. "Get back to town," he told the man jerkily, "and lose yourself for a couple days. Not a word about this to anybody, understand?"

The other did not bother to reply.

Deane crossed the ridge, riding west. His objective was a point on the old coulee trail running from the Cross 8 to Granite Basin. So great was his haste to get there that he was stung to annoyance at the return of that creepy sensation of being watched.

"Who's got any idea what I'm up to?" he argued with himself. "It can't be Robuck—I made dead sure of him. Has Mickle put a man to checkin' up on me?"

The thought angered him still further, till he put it away from him. Believing as he did that Deane had coolly murdered one partner, Dunc would have no occasion to doubt his willingness to dispose of the second.

A moment later, threading the brush, he drew in with a jerk, sitting rigid. Was that a horse he had heard? He listened keenly, his eyes probing. The evening silence was unbroken. Starting on, he flushed a big rabbit. He laughed lowly in sheer relief.

"My nerves are jittery," he told himself. "Even a jack rabbit scares me tonight."

Arriving at the old coulee, he paused at its edge to scan the trail below. Faintly white, it wound down through the brush—deserted, as far as he could see in either direction. Tension caught him up afresh. Was he in time? It had been no part of his plan to allow Virginia to ride to Granite Basin tonight, where even now Smoke Devlin must be laying in ambush. His intention was to intercept the girl on the trail as if by accident, learn ostensibly for the first time where she was going, give the lie to his own ruse, and start with her toward Flathead, where, he could safely declare to her, Robuck had been all afternoon.

Putting his pony down the bank, he rode up to the trail, where he sought the fresh tracks which would tell him that the girl had already passed. There were none. It reassured him. At the same time, darkness was coming on swiftly; he would have to watch closely in order not to miss her. He decided to wait in the trail, and, at the first sound of her coming, start toward her.

Sitting there, he planned the story he would tell her—how he had picked up a lead that day and followed it for hours, only to have it pinch out. When they met he would be on his way back to town. . . . No, that wouldn't do, either. He had to know that Robuck had remained in Flathead. Perhaps if he said that Robuck had started him off a couple of hours before—

"Damn it all!" he broke off nervously. "She's taking a long time to get here!"

Night had come, softened with high stars. Searching it attentively, he was caught up again by that nagging sensation of a nearby presence. Growling in his throat, he yanked his bronc off the trail, threading the brush at one side. He would hear Virginia's pony on the trail when she came; but this other, it seemed more than likely, would give no warning of its coming.

Had he known in what direction the striking menace lay, he would have challenged it harshly. But he did not know. It pressed in on all sides, screaming its silent warning along his nerves. As he drew his gun, the physical act itself seemed to snap him back to a sane balance. Cursing lowly, he thrust the gun back in the leather.

On the instant, a flat report rang out across the desolation. He felt a numbing blow on his left shoulder, reeled in the saddle. Desperately he threw up his own gun. He had caught the flash, which seemed to have come from the coulee rim. Firing with lightning rapidity, he stitched a circle of slugs around the spot from which that flash had come.

But for the weakness which struck at him, he would have jumped his bronc that way, run down the man who had dry-gulched him. But as his gun sagged, shock paralyzed him. Sliding out of the saddle feet first, he reached the ground, clung to the horn with his good hand, and, leaning there, listened as his assailant, apparently untouched, thrashed away through the brush.

Making sure that his bronc would stand, Deane staggered a step and sank heavily on the ground. He knew he was in a fix. The circumstances of his predicament knifed through him.

Although his wound bled freely, he felt sure he could make it to town—get there somehow, reach a doctor. But there was the girl. She must be headed off from riding into a scorpion's nest of ruthless outlaws. He *had* to wait for her!

Yet the minutes passed, and she did not come. What had happened? According to the messenger's word, it should have been no time at all after Jack reached the coulee trail before Virginia came pounding that way, her fears driving her ever faster. Clutching his wounded shoulder, Deane gulped and considered the possibilities.

Had she heard the shooting and swerved aside? Had her father, perhaps, met her while she was starting out and turned her back? He refused to consider this last possibility for a moment, both because it was an easy out, and because it would render innocuous his entire plan for this night. And yet, what else could have taken place?

Sweat started out on his brow. "If I stay here much longer, I'm a goner," he groaned. "I've given her twenty minutes—maybe half-an-hour. If I wait too long, and she don't find me, nobody else may ride this way for days!"

Yet it was not his own situation alone which harassed him. He was genuinely afraid for the girl. He had no illusions concerning what would happen to her if she found her way uninterrupted to Granite Basin. To do him credit, he would not have counted the cost to himself, could he have been sure of saving her from that fate. But the bitter knowledge beat in upon him that he could do nothing; that circumstance had outwitted him.

"My God!" he panted. "She won't come this way at all! She's gone by way of Alder Canyon—there's not a chance of stoppin' her!"

He had crawled to the trail so that she could not miss him when she came. Now his bronc stood a hundred feet away in the brush, and he had to reach it. Gritting his teeth, he started. More than once, crawling on hands and knees, with his left arm dragging, he pitched forward on his face as faintness struck at him. Reality receded; nothing existed save the fight to win back to his bronc. When he reached it, ebbing vitality seemed purposeless. He lay long, gathering his strength for the effort required to get to his feet.

That done, he fought off the giddy waves which threatened to engulf him; it was five minutes before he managed to get boot in a stirrup. And, pulling himself up, he lay over the saddle for another rest. Finally he was up. Fishing the reins to him, he turned toward the trail, weakly digging the spurs in.

Once out of the coulee, he headed the bronc toward

Flathead. Slumping in the saddle, his good hand clamped on the horn, he grimly faced the longest and hardest ride of his life.

After an early supper, his efforts still unfruitful, Robuck turned his thoughts toward the Cross 8. The ache in his heart was no easier. It seemed to him that Red remained at his side in spirit, no matter what he did or where he went. Suddenly he wanted to talk to Virginia. She would understand how he felt; he would find some comfort in her company.

A cursory hunt failed to turn up Jack Deane. No one had seen him for several hours. Robuck frowned. Probably he would find Deane awaiting him when he arrived at the Cross 8. Without further delay, he got up his bronc and set out for the ranch.

It was almost dusk when he arrived. Dale Barron emerged to the porch as he dismounted. The rancher stared.

"Robuck?" he managed, gruffly. "Wal, that's danged queer! I thought yuh was banged up—and a long ways from here!"

Robuck caught his excitement. "What do you mean?" he queried swiftly. "Nothing has happened to me. Did you hear that something had?"

Barron sat down abruptly in a handy chair. "My—girl did," he got out with difficulty. "My Gawd! So that's how it is!" He had gone gray.

Robuck was at his side in an instant. "Speak up, man!" he cried. "What do you know about this—and what did Virginia hear? Where is she?"

Dale's eyes were dulled with pain. "Robuck, an hour ago Ginie got a note that said you was layin' bad wounded, out at the Granite Basin line-camp. It asked her to come to you."

"And she went?" Robuck's clipped words were sharp.

"Right off," Barron assented heavily. "I wasn't here when the note come, or I'd have gone with her."

For a moment there was silence. Each read in the eyes of the other the knowledge of what had happened. Nothing was needed to point out the trap which had been laid for the girl.

Robuck swung abruptly toward the steps. He paused. "How long ago did you say she left?" he bit out.

"Dorrie says better'n three-quarters of an hour ago," Barron told him. "Robuck—if you're goin' out there yuh better take Borage and two-three of the boys along. Yuh may need 'em!"

Robuck yanked his cinches tight without immediate response. "Thanks, Barron," he said, his face colorless as he swung into the saddle; "but I'll have a better chance out there—and so will Virginia—if I go it alone!"

The reference to the delicacy of his daughter's predicament was a telling argument with Dale. He had no more to say on the subject. Weak and trembling, he got out: "Fer Lord's sake, don't lose no time! My little girl—"

Robuck heard none of it. He had whirled his bronc and jammed home the spurs. The mad clatter of hoofs struck out of the yard toward the old coulee trail as he rocketed into the night.

XV: *A Man's Game*

THROUGH Alder Canyon the going was so bad that Virginia had no time to think. She had taken this trail, with its switch-backs and its dangerous turns, only once before. That had been in daylight, and, shuddering, she had determined never to come this way again. But tonight, visioning the long miles between her and the spot where Bill Robuck lay wounded, she had thought only of speed.

More than once she was forced to slip out of the saddle and lead the way down some sliding shale slope, the pony all but trampling her. At last she won to the boulder-strewn canyon floor. Threading its length and emerging on the range, she gave heed once more to her half-frantic thoughts.

There had been a hundred imperative queries in her mind when she started out. What had happened? Was Robuck as seriously wounded as the note seemed to imply? Had it been in connection with the rustlers—with her brother's murder? These things had leaped to her brain. But now her blood beat in unison with a single strong pulse of necessity: To reach Robuck's side, to do what she could for him.

She realized too late that she had brought nothing with her. She would have to depend on what she found at the Granite Basin camp. That man who had brought his note, then ridden on for the doctor, must already have done what he could. She tried to take comfort in the fact that Robuck could write; yet the fact that he was wounded at all did something queer to her breathing. It was like slow suffocation, for which decisive action was the only relief.

With no false modesty in her make-up, in a few flashing thoughts she admitted all that Robuck meant to her. Much more than she had dreamed, before events had brought it crashing in upon her. But it was not his lean good-looks, his virile manhood, his undeniable intelligence alone, which moved her. Some remembered quality in his grave gray eyes had power to put a compulsion on her, so that his will became hers.

That was what that note of his had meant to her. Had he not asked her to come, she would yet have understood his desire. She would rather have died than to ignore the summons.

The trail through the brush led up to the rim of Granite Basin. Scarcely conscious of the wind whipping her face and her shoulders, the flying foam of her pony, she drew in momentarily at a point from which she could see the line-camp. The sod-roofed log cabin, a mere blot far out in an unbroken field of gray, was dark.

Something clutched at her then: some unnameable dread. She struck in the spurs recklessly, intent on getting to the cabin without delay. Lengthening its stride, the pony flashed through the brush.

Then, without the slightest warning, came disaster. Its leg plunged in a gopher hole, the horse screamed and somersaulted, throwing the girl far. Brush broke her violent fall, but could not prevent the nasty gash she got from a stub. Her senses wildly reeling, she lost consciousness.

Off to the right, at the moment the luckless pony crashed down, harsh cries, a challenge, rang out.

"What was 'at, Al?"

"What's the rannickyboo, there?"

Broncs plunged forward. Guns glinted faintly. A rider jerked to a halt at the thrash of the down horse.

"Cripes! The dang fool fell off!" this man yelled. "Spread out, you rannies! He's here in the brush some 'eres!"

They scattered like the sudden bursting of a bomb, hawlike with the expectation of blazing shots. But no shot came. A moment later one of their number cried: "Here he is! He's out cold!" He leaped to the ground, knelt in the shadows. When he rose, a burden in his arms, he met the others with an amazed gasp.

"It ain't him at all, Buff! It's some gal, so help me!"

Ogle cursed. "You shore of that? . . . Wal, get 'er down to the cabin, you and Roy. And put that hoss out of its misery." He swept the brush around them keenly at the shot. "The rest of you birds spread out again," he snapped. "This ain't what we're here for!"

A few minutes later, Roy Olds paused in the door of the line cabin. "Smoke?" he grunted. "Light a light in here."

Devlin, alone in the place, moved in the darkness without reply. A match rasped; the wick of a lantern caught, blazed up. The outlaw turned. He looked at the burden in Olds' arms, then stared quickly at him and Al.

"A girl!" he jerked out gruffly. He moved forward to have a look at her, and Olds looked too. He snorted, but his face remained passive.

"Shore. Yuh know who she is—old Barron's daughter," he said.

But Devlin, his lined, strong face intent, was examining the girl's pale features and then the bad scalp wound she had received.

"She took a hell of a bang," he mused, lips pursed. "Bring her over here and lay her down."

Olds deposited her on the bed. Devlin moved the lantern so that its light shone on her injury; then he threw a stern look at the men.

"Yuh damn fools!" he said softly. "Who took a shot at her?"

"Nobody!" Al answered hastily. "She took a header, Smoke."

Devlin grunted, turning back to the girl. He set about doing what he could for her, his thoughts busy. He had not asked how she came here, although the question had struck him immediately. Now, light was breaking.

He had received word simply that Bill Robuck would be at Granite Basin tonight, and had wondered how it would be arranged. A trick, probably—some bait which would be sure to lure the detective. This girl was the bait, the outlaw suddenly knew; and his lip curled.

"Mebby Robuck is sweet on her," he thought to

himself; "but damn the rat who'd drag a woman into anything like this!"

His face grim, he looked up as Roy Olds and Al started to leave. "Hold on," he stopped them, and thought a moment. Then he nodded. "When Robuck comes," he continued, "let him come on to the cabin. I'll handle him."

"Sure. But, Smoke, he's—that girl—"

"I said I'll take care of it!" Devlin cut him off, almost fiercely.

The two muttered an assent. Turning, they went out into the night.

Nearing Granite Basin, Robuck was cocked for trouble. He had hurled his bronc over the miles at a killing pace, with a mounting anger which strung him taut, his eyes flashing and violence in his shoulders. Long since, it had struck him that the trap into which Virginia had ridden was less for her benefit than for his own. He did not hesitate. There was nothing in him but scorn for men who would resort to such tactics. He expected in one sharp lesson to teach them what trouble meant.

Reaching the Basin rim, he slowed, sweeping the sage with an acute perception. No challenge rang out. He pushed doggedly on, jaws clamped—waiting for the first warning sound. Below him he caught a faint glimmer of light from the cabin. His heart leaped. For an hour he had been harried with the fear that when he arrived here, the place would be a dark and silent ambush, from which the bait had been safely removed.

Now, suddenly, his feeling was different. He felt sure that Virginia was there. The knowledge impelled him forward, with faint surprise that no sudden gunfire stabbed the night, no shadowy men loomed up to block his way.

A hundred yards from the cabin he drew up in the brush. Tethering his bronc, he stole on silently, every sense alert, his gun in his hand.

No dark figure stood guard at the cabin. He knew, because he circled it before he drew near. Warned by the ease of his approach, yet thrust forward by a necessity stronger than prudence, he reached the log wall, followed it to the door and paused there, arrested by what he saw.

On the blankets covering the crude bed lay Virginia. Kneeling beside her, working at her injury with clumsy but gentle fingers, was Smoke Devlin. Except for these two, the cabin was empty.

Robuck had made no slightest sound; yet so keenly attuned were the outlaw's senses that he abruptly paused. He made no quick move. Only his head turned as his eyes swung to the tall man in the door. Giving the bandage on the girl's head a last tuck, he got to his feet as Robuck moved forward.

The girl had regained consciousness under Devlin's ministrations. At the turn of his head, his glance intent, she looked also—gave a low cry.

"Bill!"

He had eyes only for her then. Sinking beside her, he took the hand she extended; tried to answer her brave smile. Something passed swiftly between them which no words could have conveyed; then, with the consciousness of what this room contained for them, what it all meant, the moment was gone.

"Are you all right?" he queried, quickly.

"Yes. My horse fell with me." Her words were steady. "But you, Bill—"

His actions answered the questions which had driven her here. Hardening even as he straightened, he shot a look across at Devlin like a steel bar. Curt words whipped out of him.

"Using women now, eh?"

Smoke returned his look without heat. Both men were so tall that they dwarfed this room, gave it the feeling of being crowded, and of something more.

"Forget it, Robuck," the cool reply dropped. "And put up yore gun. If yo're here, it's because I let yuh come . . . This is none of my doin'."

Menace flashed between them like the stroke of unseen lightning. Robuck's big shoulders were frozen with expectancy.

"You're here, waiting," he pointed out flatly. "It don't look like you didn't know what was going on, Devlin." And yet the level regard of the outlaw puzzled him. Nothing in that look said that Devlin felt responsibility for the situation; but rather the contrary.

Robuck turned to Virginia. "Why did you come here?" he asked.

"The man brought your note," she answered. "A note saying that you were here, wounded—asking me to come. I came at once."

"I sent no note." Robuck's unforgiving stare darted

to Devlin. "When I heard of it I thought—and I still do—that I knew where it came from!"

Smoke shrugged, unmoved.

"When I'm lookin' for you, Robuck, I'll come head on, and come a shootin'," he said coldly. "You're in one business and I'm in another. But I don't fight women. I didn't write no note."

There was a sting of rebuke in his tone that carried the conviction of truth.

"I have the note here," Virginia put in quickly.

"Let me see it," said Robuck colorlessly, without taking his eyes off Devlin.

She fumbled in her waist, drew out a crumpled paper. He took it, smoothed it out, and ran his glance down the writing. Before he had read two lines, something within him came to a dead stop. For an instant his brain refused to function, to accept this incredible truth. But, his blood running cold, he knew that he could not be mistaken. Only one person in the world could be responsible for the hand-writing of this note, and that person was Jack Deane!

Suddenly aware of Devlin's shrewd eye on him, Robuck called up all his will-power to dissemble the cost to him in realization of the truth. His face wooden, he slowly tore the note to shreds.

"You can't—tell anything from it?" Virginia asked anxiously.

Distrusting speech at that moment, Robuck simply shrugged. He was striving to force his wits back to the matter in hand. Whatever its cause, it was serious enough still.

"What's to be done about her?" he asked the outlaw abruptly, nodding toward Virginia.

Devlin's answer surprised even himself. "You better get her home, Robuck. There won't be a hand raised to stop yuh."

There was not a chance in the world of nailing the man now, and Robuck knew it. Moreover, he counted Virginia's safety more than a fair exchange for the opportunity.

"Will you be able to ride now?" he asked her.

"I think so."

Taking this for assent, Devlin moved toward the door. "Get yore bronc," he told Robuck dryly. "I'll get one up for the girl."

A few minutes later they met before the cabin. Devlin led a pony bearing Virginia's saddle. Robuck helped her to mount. Swinging astride, in his turn, he paused, looking down at the outlaw.

"This is mighty white of you, Devlin," he said shortly. "But don't get the idea it changes a thing between us."

"Not a thing," Smoke grunted laconically. He stared up with flinty, quizzical eyes. "All the same," he added shrewdly, "it might pay yuh to look a little closer to home for the double-cross bein' worked on yuh, Robuck."

He stepped back. Without more words, they started away. Neither spoke as they rode out of the Basin and took the old coulee trail. Once they felt safely beyond Devlin's reach, however, the girl broke the silence with a question.

"What did he mean when he said that?"

"I don't know," Robuck told her, the necessity to lie making him brief. Pursing his own thoughts with a bitter inevitability, he was scarcely aware that she glanced at him anxiously from time to time.

As clearly as print he read what had taken place, both now and in the past. Like a key turning in its lock, the note had opened the door upon the terrible truth.

"Jack's been working against us from the beginning," he told himself grimly. "He killed Red—he tried to get me. God!"

But a hitch came in his thinking here. Remembering Deane's own badly-dissembled interest in Virginia, he found it impossible to believe the other would put her in the position of danger in which he had found her. Treacherous, Jack might be—but that? Stirring restlessly in the saddle, he asked abruptly:

"How did you come to the Basin?"

She told him.

"That's not the regular way, is it?"

"No, this is. Alder Canyon is harder, but shorter."

Robuck decided that Deane had intended using her as a decoy, then intercepting her on this trail and removing her from danger. His lips stiffened at the inscrutable pattern fate had followed. Had the girl taken the easier way to Granite Basin, he might himself now be dead.

Slowly there built up in him a terrible anger against Deane; an anger which left him coolly deliberate, but resigned. He remembered that at their last talk, Deane had spoken of going to the Cross 8. Moreover, having missed Virginia on the trail, Jack would be almost certain to go to the ranch to learn what had become of her. Unconsciously, he pushed his bronc to a quicker pace.

Lights burned at the ranch. Dale Barron paced the porch nervously. At the sound of hoofs, he came hastily forward.

"Who is that?" he demanded impellingly. And then, making out a small, tired silhouette: "Ginie! Thank God!" A great sigh burst out of him.

Catching her in his arms as she slipped down, he turned to Robuck with a tremulous smile masking the shock of his relief.

"Boy, I can't name what I owe yuh—!"

"Is Deane here?" Robuck cut him off, grimly.

"Deane? Why, no! He ain't even been here."

Robuck's iron frown was hidden.

Dorrie, bustling out of the house at that moment, took charge of Virginia in her tyrannical way. In no time, the girl was inside and being cared for.

Robuck explained briefly to Dale what had taken place, omitting his knowledge of Deane's part in it. The rancher was amazed, but there could be no doubt of his deep appreciation. When Robuck tried to cut the talk short, saying he must get to Flathead, the other told him: "Don't run off. Ginie wants to see yuh before yuh go."

Robuck hesitated, then turned inside. He found Virginia in the front room. Her clear gaze met his wooden look, then dropped to his hat, still in his hand.

"Must you go?" she said. "Bill, I haven't thanked you for what you did for me—"

"Any man would have done as much," he told her. "Even Devlin had the decency to do what he could."

"Yes. You were—mistaken about him, weren't you?"

Robuck admitted as much. He had been more than a little surprised by the attitude of the outlaw; had been forced to draw a different picture of him in his mind. But as the talk ran on, he found his thoughts fixed on the girl herself. This night's events had served to show him what she meant to him—and it was much.

For all that, any exchange of sentiment between them now seemed incongruous. Things had gone too hard with him; and they had gone hard with her too, with the death of her brother and her father's difficulties. He supposed he'd ride out of her life, when the time came, the same as he had ridden into it. He found it hard to face, but he could see nothing else.

For her part, she read in his flat-lipped, expressionless countenance how bleak life had become for him, with the loss of the partner with whom he had ridden so long. So firm was his control that she did not dream that, in the knowledge of Deane's treachery, he had received a second blow almost as serious—that suddenly he stood alone against the forces of evil which surrounded them all.

Robuck made his excuses at length and turned his face toward Flathead with a leaden heart. The hardest duty of his life lay before him, yet it must be met. Reaching town, he put up his bronc and turned toward the hotel. Jack was not in the lobby. Robuck turned to the clerk. "Deane come in yet?" he queried.

"Why—why, yeah. That is, he's over to Doc Peterson's office, Robuck. Gettin' patched up."

Robuck hardened, sensing something unusual. "What do you mean?" he snapped.

"Deane showed up a couple hours ago with a slug in his shoulder," the man told him. "I heard he got bushwhacked."

Robuck waited for no more, starting for the doctor's office. Arriving there, he pushed in to find Deane, white-faced, lying on the couch with his shoulder bound up. Jack's eyes widened when he saw Robuck. But he waited for the other to speak.

"What happened to you?" Robuck grunted, his expression wooden.

"I got plugged on the Cross 8 trail," Deane managed, with what passed for a grin. "I was afraid you'd get it too. Where were you?"

"I did pretty nearly get it," said Robuck grimly. Sensing a new set-up here, he determined to play his part. Except that he failed to say he had recognized the handwriting in the note which had lured Virginia to Granite Basin, he told exactly what had taken place.

It appeared that even this blunt rehearsal of his treachery did not faze Deane. He listened inscrutably to the end and then said, with a well-simulated shudder:

"That was a close call, all right!"

"Closer than I expect to run into again for a while,"

Robuck admitted. "But how about you? Did you see who it was who shot you?"

"No, I saw the flash and fired back. That's all I know." Deane turned his face away slightly, having a hard time of it with his painful thoughts.

Robuck, watching him, believing that here lay the man who had shot his own friend, coldly thought: "I'm right about you, all right! It don't make you feel at all good to have things backfire like they have to-night—and you show it."

But along with the deep, ineradicable hurt Jack had dealt him, a thin, persistent question irked him. Who, in the line-up of events as he had pictured them, could have been responsible for the slug Doc had taken out of Deane's shoulder? With Jack secretly on the side of the outlaws, it could not have been one of their number. That was the puzzle that faced him. How did this shooting fit into the picture?

XVI: *"You Killed Him!"*

WHAT he had learned gave Robuck plenty to think about. At the same time, just how Jack Deane fitted into the case he was attempting to build was not at all clear to him. From the events at Granite Basin he drew certain knowledge that Deane had a contact with the outlaws. How had that connection been established, and how did it work?

Riding to Flathead, sick at heart, he had been sorely tempted to accuse Jack flatly and end by throwing him off. Surprised to alertness once more by what he found, however, his better judgment persuaded him to change his mind. With Deane as deeply involved as his actions proved him to be, it would be folly to toss away the opportunity for further investigation thus presented.

His fellow-feeling for Deane was as effectually dead as if it had never been. Jack had wanted it that way, and now he had it. Robuck meant to watch him as narrowly as he would a poisonous reptile, although nothing offered until Deane should have gotten on his feet again.

In the meantime, there was this other baffling problem to be considered. There being no reason for evasion here, beyond concealment of his suspicions, Robuck spoke his mind, in Deane's room in the hotel the following morning, with apparent frankness.

"What will you be doing now?" Jack inquired, from his bed.

"I'm going to try and find out what's in the background, here," Robuck replied, gazing down at him thoughtfully. "Whoever it was who killed Red and shot you and had a try at me, it's plain enough that we'll have him to deal with till we put him away. I propose to do just that."

"You got any ideas?"

"I've turned it over in my mind. It's clear to me that it's some lone wolf. Devlin's out, or he never would've let me get away when he had me. Who, then? Is it Daggett, Broke Horan—or some gent we haven't got a line on? I don't know, but I aim to find out."

"I hope you have some luck," said Deane fervently. "But look out this dry-gulcher don't pot you while you're looking for him!"

"That joke is nothing to laugh at," said Robuck grimly, turning to go. From the door, he said: "I'll be away four or five days. It'll be that long before you get around."

Their glances crossed, apparently saluting, really measuring.

"So long," said Jack.

Robuck started off without delay. Daggett was the man on whom his immediate suspicions had fastened. He determined to run the man to earth and learn, once and for all, what his real status was. That someone besides Deane himself had shot Red he did not really believe; but it was possible. Certainly it had not been Deane who had taken a shot at him that night on the

Cross 8. It was reasonable to suppose that the same man who had done that had succeeded in potting Deane. Daggett was the only man Robuck could place who had such freedom of movement.

"We'll see," he nodded to himself.

For three days he followed an endless trail. Not once during that time did he lay eyes on Daggett; which was the more queer in that Robuck had queried Dunc Mickle as to the man's whereabouts before he started out, and the banker had been explicit. Daggett had been seen, of course; he actually had been where Mickle had said, and gone on. Where he would go next no puncher could tell, for Daggett talked little and never discussed his movements.

His elusiveness alone would have been more than enough to arouse Robuck's suspicions. On the third day of his pursuit, he believed himself to be drawing up on Daggett. Twice he was told that the latter had been seen drifting toward the Elk Crossing country. He rode there, to call at several ranches, where, to his chagrin, Daggett hadn't been seen at all.

Camping alone that night, he went on in the morning in the hope that he would cut the man's trail suddenly. He was sure now that Daggett was dodging and doubling with deliberate intent to evade.

Midday found him near Elk Crossing, with no change in his luck. He rode in to Hank's hotel for a meal. Eating dinner in the dining-room, deserted save for himself, he was trying to devise some means of obtaining quick results when the sun-baked, dreaming silence outside the hotel shattered to the crash of a gun.

Robuck's head came up with a jerk. On the instant, he slipped out of his chair and reached the outer door in half-a-dozen swift strides. What he saw was something which he had least expected to see.

At the corner of Blascom's store, across the way, stood Daggett, a smoking gun in his hand, a hard glint in his eye. Near the hotel window, a man lay sprawled face down, a pool of blood slowly spreading under him. There was a gun near his hand which had dropped as he fell.

Robuck took that in in a glance, and his keen look flicked to Daggett once more. The latter came forward nonchalantly, blowing the smoke from his gun-barrel and replacing the spent cartridge.

"Howdy, Robuck," he nodded.

"Daggett, what happened here, anyhow?" Robuck put the flat question, watching every move the other made.

"I seen yuh eatin', over here, from the store," was Daggett's cool response. "I was comin' over to talk to yuh. No sooner'n I got out the door, I saw this bushwhackin' skunk peekin' in the window at yuh. It wouldn't a done no good fer me to sing out. He had a bead on yuh, and would've mebby let yuh have it anyway—he looked like he shore meant business. So I took a hand the only way I knowed how. What you see," he concluded dryly, glancing down at the dead man, "is the result."

Robuck was amazed. "He had me covered from the

window, you say?" he queried—but it was largely to gain time. He had no doubt that Daggett was telling the truth, and his judgment of the man underwent a violent wrench.

"He shore did," Daggett nodded. "Who is he, anyhow? What's his grudge against yuh?" The query sounded almost anxious.

For answer, Robuck leaned down and turned over the dead man. He uttered a cry, stiffening, as he found himself gazing into the unshaven face and glazed eyes of Lafe Rash, whom he had last seen escaping from the Wagonspoke court-house in the Sweetwater Basin of Wyoming.

Daggett was watching him interestedly. "Know him, do yuh?"

"I should say I do!" In a few words Robuck explained Rash's identity. Evidently Rash had drifted up here, seeking sanctuary, and had somehow learned of the presence of his old enemies.

Daggett nodded in a relieved way. "Uh-huh," he grunted. "That explains a lot."

For his part, Robuck was seeing clearly a good deal which had confused him before. Lafe Rash, he knew suddenly, was the man who had bushwhacked Jack Deane. He's the man who shot at me that other time, and he was bent on finishing the job today," he mused.

"Daggett, I owe you something for this," he said slowly. "This man shot Deane a few days ago. It wouldn't surprise me if he was responsible for Red Lefler's death." It occurred to him that this was the logical solution to that mystery; that Deane, whatever his desires, would not have dared to shoot his partner as openly as Red had been shot.

He turned as Hank Blascom blustered out of the store, storming and ranting over the promiscuous shooting which was becoming so common about his premises. Only the fact that he knew both Daggett and Robuck to be Association detectives calmed him down. With the story explained to him, he departed, grumbling, to have a man look after Rash's disposal.

Robuck and Daggett repaired to the hotel dining-room while the former finished his meal. Completely satisfied at last that the other was on the square, Robuck spoke freely.

"Daggett," he began; "after I told you who and what Lafe Rash was, you said an odd thing. You said 'That explains a lot,' as though it cleared up things in your mind. Is that right?"

Delaying a moment, Daggett replied deliberately: "I was wonderin' if you caught that . . . Robuck, yuh ain't near as deep into this case as yuh think yuh are. There's things goin' on here yuh don't even dream of. I ain't sayin' what I know about it," he proceeded, lowering his voice; "but I will say I never did savvy all this shootin at you fellers. Fittin' this Rash into the picture the way he belongs, clears things up a lot."

Robuck eyed him quizzically, wondering just how much he knew. "Well," he observed, "there's nothing mysterious about this rustling. It just goes on, and that's all there is to it."

Daggett demurred cautiously. "Don't be so shore about that," he warned. "Did it ever occur to yuh that all the ranches are not bein' rustled—but only certain ones?"

Of course it had. But Robuck evaded the direct query. "Why should that be?" he countered.

"Figure it our fer yoreself—if yuh can," Daggett replied, waggling his head. "I'm jest sayin' yuh ain't seen all of this business by a long shot."

"I know a few things, myself," Robuck admitted thoughtfully. "I'll confess that I've changed my mind about you. What's the matter with throwing our evidence together and seeing what we get?"

Daggett smiled, shaking his head. "Thanks," he declined, and added candidly: "I reckon I can crack this case before you do."

"We're both working for the Association," Robuck reminded.

"Are we?" Daggett's dry smile widened. When Robuck waited, he could not resist saying: "Hirin' a man is a swell way fer certain ones to keep him tagged. Mebby yuh never thought of that."

It was a new idea, and one which Robuck found worthy of consideration. He looked at Daggett with a new respect. The man was as shrewd as he was cagey.

"What's your particular interest in working alone?" he inquired.

"Wal, mebby that's my way of insurin' results." Daggett mused for a moment. "I ain't givin' anything away," he resumed, "by admittin' that I aim to stand behind old Barron in this deal. He done me a real favor, a few years ago. I reckon Dale's forgot it, but I ain't. I've seen him lose his boy through this trouble—I don't aim to watch him lose his ranch."

It was so much different an answer from what Robuck had expected that he found his respect increasing. His interest in his companion was genuine as, leaving the hotel, they swung up on their broncs.

"Where are you headed?" he asked.

"Wal—" Daggett hesitated. "Where you goin'?"

"Back to town."

Daggett shook his head. "Not fer me. I'll side you far's the Dry Shoshone, though."

They rode that far together. There, Daggett turned off, lifting his hand in an easy gesture of farewell. Watching him ride away, Robuck grinned. He knew now why Daggett was so hard to find. The man disliked letting anyone know his movements, even those he felt he could trust.

It was midafternoon when Robuck reached Flathead. He went at once to the sheriff's office and acquainted Shandler with what had happened at Elk Crossing, putting Daggett in the clear by offering to produce proof of Lafe Rash's identity. Since Rash was unquestionably a rustler, Shandler was disinclined to become excited about the matter.

Later Robuck found Jack Deane in the lobby of the hotel. Jack was talking to someone as Robuck entered, and when this man turned to glance furtively toward the door, the latter saw that he was Spokey Withers. Seeing himself observed, Spokey said something to Deane in a low voice and moved off.

It gave Robuck pause, but only for a moment. Deane

did not immediately see him. When he did, he looked up with sudden interest, apparently untroubled by anything.

"Well!" he said. "Back, eh? What luck did you have?"

Robuck, avoiding any reference to Spokey, told him about the reappearance of Lafe Rash, and the man's equally sudden demise. Deane's face brightened at the information.

"Rash, eh? That's a surprise!" he exclaimed. "He's the bird that killed Red," he went on with conviction; "and the one who got me. And he's the one who tried to get you knocked off out at Granite Basin too, I'll wager!"

Robuck shrugged. "He knew a whole lot more about what's going on than I'd have believed he did, if that's so," he said.

"That's right," Jack concurred. "But don't forget—he's been around for quite a spell since he took that crack at you out on the Cross 8. He's had time to find out things."

This verbal sparring would have served to revive Robuck's suspicions in full force, if that were needed. With Deane's getting about once more, he realized that he must be on the watch. Moreover, there were matters awaiting his consideration here in town. He had not forgotten Red's having seen Spokey Withers riding away from Smoke Devlin's hideout. With the man in touch with Deane, he believed he had found the link between Jack and the outlaws.

Besides that, there was Dunc Mickle to be evaluated

afresh. Robuck had never liked Mickle. He had had his suspicions of him before, only to discard them after a time. Where could Dunc possibly fit into the puzzle?

Although Jack Deane would have said that Robuck took it easy that evening, the latter kept a watchful eye on both him and Mickle. He knew when Dunc ate his supper and who he talked to before going back to spend the evening at his desk. He knew every man Deane himself talked to before turning in early, and that Spokey Withers had not again put in an appearance.

This went on the next day. Robuck's interest in Spokey was growing. He wanted to know more about Withers; but since he had disappeared, the simplest way of picking him up would be to wait for his return. If Robuck's suspicions were not wholly unfounded, Spokey would be certain to show up somewhere in Deane's vicinity before long.

The day passed without incident. Calling on his patience, Robuck waited. The evening was a replica of the previous one. The following morning, Wade Shandler accosted him to say that he had made a trip to Elk Crossing, where he confirmed the story Robuck had told. As far as he was concerned, the sheriff added, the shooting of Lafe Rash was a closed account.

Before noon, however, there were developments which made Robuck wonder whether someone else was not vitally concerned. Standing in the doorway of the Ox-Yoke, he watched a puncher jog down the street and head for the sheriff's office. His eye fixed. The man was leading a pack-horse, and over the animal's back lay a canvas-swathed burden whose shape Robuck all too readily recognized.

Dropping his cigarette, he started over there. When he arrived, the puncher had unfastened his burden and was opening it for Shandler's benefit. Reaching Shandler's side, Robuck leaned over—and found himself staring at the dead face of Daggett.

"Good Lord!" he jerked out. "How did this happen?"

The puncher explained. He had been combing the hills above the Dry Shoshone for sleepers, he said, and had come across Daggett hanging to a tree and filled with slugs.

Shandler shook his head over the story in a puzzled way, staring at the gruesome sight. "They cert'nly went to work on him, whoever 'twas!" he grunted.

For his part, Robuck was thrown into confusion once more. He had believed that with Lafe Rash's identification, he had solved the problem of the mysterious slayings; and now here was ghastly evidence of another such killing.

Walking away, he set himself a number of pregnant questions. Who could have hated Daggett sufficiently to have treated him in this fashion? Daggett had hinted that he knew more even than Robuck guessed about some secret power dominating the range. Had he met his death because he knew too much, and gave himself away? And to whom?

He was still pondering these things when, in early afternoon, word that he was wanted at the bank immediately, reached him at the hotel.

"Okay," he told the messenger. "Tell Mickle I'll be along directly."

Even so, he remained sitting in his chair in the lobby for some minutes, turning things over. It was plain that Mickle's summons grew out of what had happened to Daggett. What would Dunc have to say on that subject? He gave it up. "There's a better way of finding out than this," he mused. Pulling himself to his feet, he headed for the bank.

Mickle lifted a flashing eye from his papers as Robuck arrived. Clearly he was on the war-path about something; and it was this unpredictable streak in him which had made Robuck question the man's sincerity from the beginning.

"What do you know about Daggett's death?" he rapped out, abruptly.

Robuck sank, uninvited, into a chair and met his sharp regard levelly. "I've heard of it. I saw his body when it was brought in. I got the same story of how he was found that Shandler heard. Why?"

Mickle's severe visage darkened at this cool response. "Yes? What else do you know about it?" he snapped impellingly.

Robuck frowned. "Mickle, I don't like your tone. What else should I know about it?"

He kept his voice even, but there was nothing idle about his words. Out of the corner of his eye he saw Wade Shandler enter the bank and turn this way. The sense of trouble suddenly strung him taut, although he did not change his position in the chair. Mickle, he knew sharply, had something up his sleeve. What was it?

Mickle fired up suddenly. "Dammit, Robuck!" he exploded vehemently, as Shandler neared. "You know plenty about it. You killed him yourself!"

Robuck half rose from his chair, his look dangerous. Then he slowly sank back. Whether or not Shandler had known this crackling accusation of murder was coming, it was impossible to tell. He looked at them both, but said nothing.

"What makes you think I would have wanted to see Daggett dead?" Robuck demanded flatly.

"He was last seen riding away from Elk Crossing in your company!" Dunc fired at him. "He was killed that same afternoon! It's known that you had no use for the man. Why, you've had words with him a couple of times, to my knowledge—"

"How would you know," Robuck cut in with deadly calm, "whether I'd ever had words with Daggett, or not?"

"Your partner, Deane, told me," said Mickle, with suave vindictiveness. "I suppose now you'll say he wasn't tellin' the truth!"

So that was it. Robuck avoided the mistake of arguing. "You're all wrong about this. I didn't kill Daggett, and I suspect you're perfectly aware of it." He turned to Shandler. "How about it, Sheriff? What's your stand in this matter?"

Shandler shook his head, gazing at Mickle in a stolidly surprised way. "We've got nothin' on this man," he pointed out matter-of-factly. "We can't hold him, if that's what yo're drivin' at. Why, Dunc, he told me himself that Daggett saved his life when he plugged that feller, Rash."

"That's his story—isn't it?" Mickle flung out angrily.

"Wall, it fits mighty well with what Blascom had to say," Shandler replied dryly.

Watching Mickle closely, Robuck saw the boiling hatred of this man. Dunc controlled it with difficulty. His next words were dogged, forceful.

"Have it your way, Shandler—though I tell you, yo're makin' a mistake! For my part, I wash my hands of him. You," he told Robuck with suppressed violence, "are fired, right now! I'll undertake to explain my action to the Association, and my reasons for it!" His bitter stare was a threat, if his words were not enough.

Robuck suddenly saw what all this had been leading up to. He got up from his chair and paused, looking down at Mickle coldly.

"This is no particular surprise to me," he said thinly. "Don't get the idea that it takes me out of this thing for a minute. I'm staying on my own!" He let that sink in. "One of the last things Daggett told me," he wound up, "was that being hired by the Association was the surest way there was of being side-tracked—so maybe I'm not losing anything!"

Dunc fired up instantly, but mastered himself, his visage apopletic. "What do you mean by that?" he spat out. Robuck only met his look, and he continued: "We'll consider that unsaid. If I hear any more of your insolent insinuations, Robuck, it'll go hard with you!"

Robuck found this scarcely worth replying to. He had thrown a jolt into Mickle, and he knew it. Turning on his heel, and nodding to Shandler, he walked out.

Later, he made a point of hunting up Deane and telling him what had occurred. Jack, listening to the entire story, raised his brows.

"Fired you, eh? You were a little hot-headed, weren't you? It's a salary, you know."

Robuck nodded. "If you look at it that way. But I don't need the Association. I'll go it alone, from here out."

There was an unspoken query in the words which Deane did not miss. His answer was casual. "Well, we all see it our own way. I'll string along with the Association for a while, if it's all the same to you."

It was so nearly what Robuck had expected to hear that he was not in the least surprised.

XVII: *Hemp Threat*

FOR sixty hours Jack Deane made no move which the most critical could condemn. Tired of a waiting game, in the bright sun of early morning Robuck swung aboard his bronc and started out of town, his thoughts fastened on the untimely death of Daggett by the surprising accusation of Dunc Mickle.

That the banker had used Daggett's murder as an excuse to fire him, he was satisfied. But why Dunc should suddenly seek a means to dispose of him was a deeper question. He had spent a restless night trying to decide in what manner he had stepped on Mickle's toes recently, without hitting on anything except an idea so fantastic that he approached it, even in the privacy of his thoughts, with considerable reserve.

In the meantime, a notion that wouldn't leave him alone was taking him back to Elk Crossing. He had gone over his meeting with Daggett with a fine-tooth comb for some clue to the reason for Daggett's killing. The one answer he always returned to was that their talk in the hotel dining-room, when the cagey Association detective had dropped the hint that he knew a good deal, had been overheard.

What there was to be gained by going back over the ground at this late date was problematical; but Robuck, in his present frame of mind, was leaving no stone unturned.

Reaching Elk Crossing, he dismounted before the hotel and entered the bar. Several drifting punchers were here, chewing the rag and taking it easy. Ordering a drink, Robuck looked them over casually but carefully. The bar-tender slid out bottle and glass, and, seeing that Robuck was alone, paused for a word or two. His idea of conversation was rather heavy humor.

"Yo're goin' to find it a job, persuadin' superstitious folks to talk to yuh, around here," was his opening gambit.

Robuck glanced at him curiously. "Why is that?"

"Wal, it's considered bad luck by some," the bartender chuckled. "If that man Daggett is any example, mebby there's somethin' in it."

"What about you?" Robuck queried easily. "Aren't you a mite worried, making so free with me?"

"Naw," the other scoffed affably. "Nobody pays me no mind."

At that moment, Robuck pivoted on an elbow resting on the bar, to glance up as a newcomer darkened the door. His nerves snapped to tension as he saw that it was Spokey Withers. But Spokey saw him almost as quickly. His shrewd, faded eyes narrowed for the space of an instant; then, suddenly changing his mind about entering, he whirled in the doorway and stepped back outside. His boots crunched hastily as he started away.

Robuck got to the door as speedily as an appearance of nonchalance would permit. He was in time to see Spokey spurring away to the south at a good clip.

The bar-keeper laughed, a husky, accordion-like wheeze in his chest, when Robuck turned back. "What'd I tell yuh?" he jibed. "That gent don't like yuh a bit. He didn't even wait to argue the matter!"

"Spokey?" Robuck smiled. "What makes you think he's got me on his mind?"

"Seen him give yuh one look and tear, didn't yuh?" The man jerked his chin downward decisively. "Ole Spokey knows what's what! To do him credit, though, I never did see the time when he craved to mingle with yuh none."

On the verge of learning something he very much wanted to know, Robuck didn't trust to words to get over the wrong impression. But his disbelieving look was sufficiently challenging.

"He was here the last time you was," the bar-tender continued explanatorily. "And he wasn't no more inclined to write yuh a letter about it than this time. I thought he'd break a neck, that other time, watchin' you and Daggett through the winder!"

"That didn't stop him from staying right here in the hotel until after we were gone," said Robuck, taking a blind shot.

"Wal—that's right," the other admitted. He turned away to serve a customer at the upper end of the bar, leaving Robuck to his thoughts.

"I wasn't far wrong," he told himself. "Somebody overheard Daggett's talk with me, all right—and that somebody was Spokey Withers!"

Drifting unobstrusively to the door, he determined to trail Spokey and learn where he was going. To mount his bronc, circle the hotel and strike out through the sage was the work of only a minute. He cut Spokey's trail close enough to the Crossing to identify it by the deep gouges and the long stride of the running pony. A couple of miles farther on, Spokey had hauled in and evidently turned to look back over his trail.

"Expecting me," Robuck mused, his lean face sobering.

It caused him to push forward with more caution from then on. Apparently the time he had spent talking with the bar-tender had been long enough, however, to persuade Spokey that he was not being followed. He went on at a more moderate pace, but it was plain that he was keeping to low ground and going to some bother to avoid the stretches across which he might have been seen for any distance.

Robuck's mind was busy as he dogged the other's tracks. If the bar-tender's words had not been enough, Spokey's actions showed that he had something to fear from Robuck. The latter nodded.

"If Daggett could talk now, he'd have plenty to say about you," he reflected.

At first he had believed Spokey more or less a hanger-on of Smoke Devlin's gang. Despite what Red Lefler had seen, Spokey spent more of his time in the cheap saloons of Flathead than anywhere else. With the exception of Jack Deane, Robuck had never seen him talking to anyone in town but down-and-outers. Now, suddenly, a new idea sprang into his mind.

"Devlin has use for a messenger," he thought. "Deane's getting in touch with him proves that. But

Spokey was around before Jack began to slip. Who else in town does Devlin need to keep in touch with?"

Whoever it was, there could no longer be much doubt that Spokey was the go-between.

Spokey's trail swung in a westerly direction from Elk Crossing and struck out with more assurance. Half-an-hour later, Robuck began to draw up on the other.

"He's heading for Mickle's S C spread," he told himself. There came back to him suddenly the ruse played on him and his partners by Rawlins, Mickle's foreman.

Shortly afterward, approaching the S C along the willow-tangled creek which passed not far from the ranch house, from where he could see without being seen, he watched Spokey jog into the yard. A moment later, Rawlins emerged from the house and the two men met and spoke after the manner of old acquaintances. Spokey didn't bother to unsaddle, looping his bridle-rein over a corral bar and tieing a loose knot. Then, still talking, he and Rawlins turned toward the house and entered it.

Robuck's expression, as he straightened up, was grim. "That settles it!" he grunted. He was certain now that Spokey was the connecting link between the outlaws and not only Rawlins, but Dunc Mickle as well.

"Mickle may not know what's going on out here," he mused on; "but it's my guess that he does. Daggett made it pretty clear that the Association was side-tracking me—but for Dale Barron's benefit, or Ike Greer's, or Cal McDonough's? Not likely, when it was Mickle who hired us!

"Mickle was mad when we snagged Broke Horan's

men and broke up the shipping from Salt Fork," he continued to sum up. "He told us to stick together. He had us sent out to the S C, here, while a raid was going on at the Cross 8. He fired me." Robuck's clinching nod was curt. "I'm beginning to see a lot."

He began to draw away from the ranch with the same caution he had used in his approach. It was no part of his intentions to over-play his hand at this stage of the game. Spokey Withers was of more value to him, at large and reasonably unsuspicious, than he could possibly be in custody.

Once safely out of sight, Robuck headed for Flathead. Believing he had solved the mystery of Daggett's murder, he found himself in better spirits than he had enjoyed for some time. While it was not certain that Spokey had himself handled the detective so summarily, certainly he was the one who, having heard Daggett's cagey intimation of knowledge at Elk Crossing, had arranged for the fate which had overtaken the man. That, more than anything else, served to persuade Robuck that the line he was working on now was far from being the wrong one.

Reaching Flathead in early afternoon, he was heading for the hotel when the sight of Wade Shandler, riding into the main street with a bound man on a horse preceding him, gave him pause. Struck by something familiar in the aspect of the prisoner, Robuck pushed forward for a better look. Suddenly his jaw dropped. He stared. The man Shandler had picked up was Broke Horan!

Other men were as quick to note what was going on.

They gathered in the street, following Shandler to the jail. Ugly looks were directed at Horan, the cattle-buyer, who had been disposing of stolen stock for the rustlers. Several cowboys applied blistering epithets to him. A rancher called gruffly across the dust: "By Gawd, now yo're doin' somethin', Shandler!"

Robuck followed to the jail. He had to push his way through the gathering which stood before the place, discussing Horan. Shandler had refused them admittance, lodging Horan in a cell, but he let Robuck in.

"Where did you pick Horan up, Shandler?" the latter queried.

"I had to go down the line forty miles or so on some routine business," was the reply. "Broke was millin' around a sidin' down there. I got a hand on his shoulder before he knowed I was around."

"Any of his friends with him?"

"Didn't seem like," Shandler responded. "I seen a lot of grins, but nobody lifted a hand to help him. He come along like a lamb."

Robuck smiled. "I got the idea, myself, that Horan wasn't any too pleased, but couldn't see what to do about it."

" 'Bout the size of it," the sheriff admitted laconically. Robuck noticed that his eye strayed again and again to the door. The crowd there seemed to increase, if anything. Voices were lifted in open condemnation of the prisoner. Broke Horan was the first of the rustlers harrying the Flathead range to be seen in town, the men captured at Salt Fork having been shipped through to Twospot for trial.

Robuck presently left the jail and went down to the hotel. He had no intention of forgetting Jack Deane, and was looking for him now. But Jack was nowhere to be found. At the stable, on inquiry Robuck learned that Deane had got up a pony with the remark that he was going to try the saddle once more. No one knew where Deane had headed, but Robuck had his own idea. Riding for the first time since his wound had healed, Jack would not get far before soreness drove him back, in any event. The only thing to be done was to await his return.

In the meantime, Robuck found his interest carried in another direction. Instead of gradually getting accustomed to the idea of Broke Horan's apprehension, Flathead was growing excited over it. More than the usual number of ranchers were in town today. They gathered in knots at hitch-rails and stable doors, talking in low tones but with evident vehemence. They shut up and waited, wooden-faced, when anyone approached who was not of their kind, but Robuck had little difficulty in determining the burden of their heated discussions.

Walking back to the jail, he was not surprised to find that Shandler was sticking there. He eyed Robuck sharply when the latter stepped in, but remained impassive.

"Shandler, it looks like the boys are workin' themselves into a lather about Horan," Robuck opened up bluntly. "It might be a good idea to get him away from here as soon as possible."

"Seventeen is the first chance I got," Shandler

grunted, his shortness betraying his knowledge of what was afoot.

"What time is that?"

"Ten after four."

Robuck shook his head. "That's an hour or so. More than time for Horan to dance himself to a standstill on thin air, with the preliminaries thrown in."

"I know it!" Shandler snapped testily. "Yuh better clear out of here yoreself, if yuh don't like the looks of things."

Robuck made no direct reply to this, but he did not leave. They were still discussing the situation when a hoarse shout from the street interrupted them.

"Hey, Shandler! Trot Horan out here. We want him!"

The sheriff sprang out of his chair with a muffled oath. His face was wrathy when he reached the door. More than two score men withstood his piercing survey.

"Who was yellin' at me?" he jerked out forbiddingly.

No one said anything. Shandler stared at them condemningly for a long moment. "I'm tired of this foolishness!" he declared. "Gwan about yore business, now, all of yuh!"

Standing at his side, Robuck noted that smiles of derision visited the faces of those who did not laugh outright. Emboldened, one of the crowd stepped forward. It was Cuff Morrell, a burly puncher for one of the northern spreads.

"Come off, Shandler!" he blurted. "Don't try to

bluff us! Toss Horan out here, before we git tired of askin'. We'll take care of 'im!"

Shandler pointed a furious finger at Cuff. "You hunt yore trouble some'eres else, Morrell, before I give yuh more'n yuh bargain for! It's yore kind that always starts somethin'! I'm tellin' yuh I won't have it!"

A number of older men were in the crowd. More were arriving steadily. A shock of deadly sobriety went over them at Shandler's blunt defiance. Ike Greer, a tall, bearded man, called attention to himself by saying loudly:

"Wall, boys—are we still talkin' this over, or are we goin' to do somethin' about it? Yuh all know what Horan is. Shandler's fixin' to ship him away and put him through the mill, where he'll go free in a month's time. *I* say we settle this business right here and now!"

Cries of agreement arose.

"Hang the rustlers!"

"Yank him outa there!"

"Give Shandler his orders!" the threatening suggestions rose on every hand. The crowd began to mill closer, excited by these outbursts.

Shandler stepped back from the door, his lined visage hardening, and grabbed up a rifle. "The first man that puts foot in this jail, goes down!" he yelled.

Robuck, grasping what impended, wasted no time in hesitations. He had seen this kind of a crowd before. Drawing his gun in a lightning movement, he put himself at Shandler's side. His icy glance roved the angry faces, and his voice was low and steady.

"Better listen to the sheriff, boys," he advised. "He means what he says, and I'm backing him up. You're not going to take Horan out and string him up, and you might as well get used to the idea. He gets his chance like any other man!"

"Who the hell are you?"

"Put up that gun!" came the ugly response. But the forward push of the crowd was halted. Those in the foreground braced themselves, measuring Robuck and Shandler calculatingly.

"Come on, feller!" someone cajoled harshly. "Yuh know we can get past yuh easy enough! Give us Horan—that's all we want!"

With Shandler muttering fiercely at his side, Robuck shook his head. "No necktie party today," he said with finality. "You're all wrong, boys. Don't make your mistake too expensive."

Even as they hesitated, Dale Barron pressed through. He took in the men in the jail door, and turned to the crowd.

"Mebby yo're a leetle hasty about this thing, boys, don't you think?" he said persuasively. "I feel the same way about this that you do; don't nobody think different—but Robuck, here, has done a lot for us all. I'm inclined to listen to him."

Argument broke out suddenly. Dale had all he could do to hold his own. In the heat of words, the tension of the moment relaxed. Shandler prudently allowed the talk to go on, knowing that each passing moment swept them further away from violence.

Wrathy yells still rose, and the crowd continued to

grow; but it became apparent that the intervention of Dale Barron had averted immediate action. Shandler slammed the door and fastened it.

"They'll have a hell of a time gettin' in here now!" he snorted. He began to collect arms of every description, disposing them handily; but a few minutes later, when they looked out again, the crowd had already begun to disperse.

The Cross 8 owner entered. "Nice work, Shandler," he complimented. "I shore thought there'd be a ruckus there fer a minute. Yuh handled it jest right."

"All the same," Robuck struck in, "I'd see to it that you get Horan out of here on seventeen, if you have to stretch a point to do it."

"I'll do that," Shandler nodded. "He'll be just nicely in time to go on trial with them other birds." He eyed Robuck levelly. "And thanks for standin' by me, Robuck. I ain't so shore I could have handled it alone."

Robuck passed it off easily. Standing alone as he did, he had been glad of the chance to make a friend of the sheriff.

"Yuh certainly do manage to keep busy," said Barron later, as the two walked away from the jail. "What's the matter with ridin' out to the ranch with me?"

Since there were a few things he wanted to learn, which he believed Dale could tell him, Robuck assented. Shortly after a large crowd saw Broke Horan off on the train in Shandler's custody, he and Barron took the Cross 8 trail.

The latter was much interested in the account of

recent happenings. It angered him that Mickle should have discharged Robuck out of hand, and he promised to do something about it. They were still discussing affairs when they reached the ranch.

Robuck was not slow to observe Jack Deane sitting on the porch in conversation with Virginia. A wave of sharp resentment went over him, leaving him hot. Had he his way, he would not allow Deane to so much as approach the girl, after what had happened. He must have revealed something of his feelings, for when he stepped up on the porch a moment later, a faint smile played about Virginia's lips as though she enjoyed his discomfiture.

"Hello, Bill," she greeted him. And to her father: "You're just in time for supper, Daddy. You don't know how you plague Dorrie by arriving at the last moment so regularly."

Deane stood up, looking, Robuck thought disgustedly, like the cat that had swallowed the canary. He adjusted his sling elaborately.

"Better stay for a bite, Deane," Barron suggested hospitably.

"Why, I—I was just ready to pull away," Jack responded. He looked at Virginia. Had she seconded the invitation, he would have remained despite Robuck's plain disfavor. But she did not. Reluctantly he wandered down to the corrals, swung awkwardly into the saddle and jogged away toward town.

Later, at the table, the talk returned to affairs in Flathead. Virginia was indignant that Robuck had been dropped by the Association. It appeared that Deane had told her about it.

"They don't know what they're doing!" she declared, her pretty eyes snapping. "Accusing Bill of murder! . . . It's a wonder that Jack Deane wasn't discharged for getting himself shot."

"Dunc Mickle's the one," her father put in. "He's changed from the way he used to be. Bit off more'n he could chew, or somethin'."

"What do you mean by that?" Robuck queried quickly. It had been his intention to ask some questions about Mickle.

"Wal, there's a lot of things that go to show," Dale replied. "He's been after me to pay the interest on my mortgage in advance, for one. Offered me a nice discount. I'd shore like to take it; but I can't afford it, the way things are."

"Why, Dad! You never told me about that," Virginia exclaimed.

"I'm tellin' you now."

Robuck's brows were raised, as he gazed across at the rancher. "Didn't you tell me once that Mickle had been easier on you? What do you suppose his object is?" he asked.

Dale shrugged. "Figure it out. Kin Barnes—he's a sheepman from over west—he told me Dunc refused to lend him ten thousand, the other day, even at eight percent. Dunc claims sheep's no investment this season, but I don't see it, myself."

From this, and from other things which Barron dropped, Robuck gathered that Mickle was hard up for cash at present. It was somewhat unusual for a man who owned a bank, and he was still turning it over in his mind when he said good-night and turned toward the corrals for his bronc.

Arriving there, he stopped as his hand, seeking the saddle-horn, met a paper tied loosely to the horn. He detached it, wondering what it could be. A moment later, striking a match, he knew.

> Thanks Robuck for helpin Broke Horan out of a jam (the note read). You got nerve like I said and I owe you one I wont forget.

The "S.D." with which the note was signed, Robuck knew at once, stood for Smoke Devlin.

"Well, I'll be damned!" he murmured, fingering the crumpled paper. "One of his crowd has been right here at the ranch while I was in the house."

XVIII: *Gun Talk*

"SOMETHIN' queer about this. Devlin's men ain't put hoof on the range for days," said Trig Borage. His leathery visage screwed up in shrewd lines. "If we'd busted the gang up some, or they was busy in some other quarter, I wouldn't think nothin' about it. But they ain't been heard of nowheres."

"It is odd," Robuck admitted. "I've noticed it, myself. But I've been expecting them to show up all of a sudden, in full war-paint."

It was a week after the capture of Broke Horan. Riding out to the Cross 8 this morning, Robuck had overtaken the ranch foreman on the trail, and they rode on together. Always the first to give credit where credit was due, Robuck was thinking of Trig as a man who kept his eyes open; for the other had put into words a circumstance which occupied no little space in his own thoughts, although no other man he had talked to had thought it worthy of discussion.

"Wall," said Borage, "showin' up sudden is their specialty. Don't yuh be so shore they won't do it yet."

Robuck smiled grimly. "You sound as if you'd learned from bitter experience," he remarked.

"Who ain't?"

With this indisputable observation, Trig, who was

not a talkative man, lapsed into reflective silence. They came presently in sight of the Cross 8. Entering the yard, Robuck saw Virginia cinching up her pony at the corrals. He left Borage and rode forward.

"Hello, Bill," she greeted him, in the same rich tone she always used. "I haven't seen you for some time."

Warmth flowed through him at this evidence that she had noticed his absence.

"I've been busy," he confessed. "Plenty busy. Is Dale home?"

She told him her father was in his office. "I suppose I can't persuade you to take a ride with me this morning?" she added casually.

Genuine regret showed in his eyes. "Gosh, I'd sure like to—" he temporized with himself.

Virginia laughed lightly. "Well, perhaps some other time, Bill. I can see by your expression how much your conscience would bother you." She laughed again in a tantalizing way, and, leaping gracefully astride her pony, before he had time to make a response, she swung across the yard and out upon the range.

Ever since their experience at Granite Basin there had been this elusive new relationship between them, in which it seemed to Robuck that she both drew him toward her, and put him away. He did not consider it coquetry; it was too much just Virginia for that; yet it puzzled him. He would have said they had traveled a long ways since their meeting on the train and the adventure in the Blackfoot desert, but in exactly what direction they had gone he could not have told.

He gazed after her for a moment, noting the swallow-like poise of her in the saddle, a furrow marking his brow. Then he turned toward the house.

Dale was just coming out of his office, the smoke of a new-lit cigar curling behind him, when Robuck entered. The rancher's face brightened.

"Wal, my boy!" he said heartily, clapping Robuck on the shoulder. "Ginie was speakin' about you this mornin'—wonderin' where you was keepin' yoreself."

"Was she?" Robuck's pleasure in the knowledge thinned off as he recalled that his coming had not interfered with her riding away. "I've stuck pretty close to Flathead, trying to work out a lead."

They emerged to the porch and sat down. Dale frowned, examining his cigar.

"Sorry to tell yuh I ain't got nowheres with the Association," he said. "I put in a word for yuh every chance I got. The members don't really believe in this Daggett charge, but they seem inclined to let Mickle run the outfit to suit himself. He's head of it, yuh know," he added.

"Thanks, Barron," Robuck told him. He smiled slowly. "I don't believe I'd join up with the Association again if I could."

"Wal, yuh won't get the chance," Dale concurred plainly. "I've tackled Mickle, and he's stiff-necked as hell. He won't budge an inch. I even quarreled with him over it." A harassed look crept into his eyes. "I dunno whether that means he'll give me trouble on my mortgage, or not."

Robuck became serious in a moment. He knew that this man was the best friend he had on the range.

"Don't carry the matter any further," he cautioned. "It isn't fair to yourself, and it isn't worth it."

"Anythin's worth it, if it'll help yuh with yore work," Dale maintained staunchly. He promised to drop the affair of Robuck's discharge only when the latter assured him that persistence might do more harm than good.

Under Robuck's guidance, the talk turned to the subject Trig Borage had broached. Barron added his bit.

"I've talked to owners up and down the range," he declared; "and they all say the same. No raids. No sight of scoutin' rustlers. . . . It's a relief to me, but not much. Devlin's doin' a job somewheres else. He'll be back."

"Yes, he'll be back."

Robuck did not voice his growing suspicion that Smoke Devlin depended on Dunc Mickle for both cooperation and protection; but he knew outlaws well enough to understand that none would lightly discard the double advantages this arrangement afforded.

Later in the morning, he swung reluctantly aboard his bronc and headed back for Flathead. Virginia had not returned. He conned the fact soberly, wondering whether his presence had simply meant nothing to her, whether she was paying him back for his own seeming neglect, or whether it was merely her way.

Arriving in town, he stabled his pony and wandered down the street with every appearance of aimless indolence. He was doubly on guard these days. He had not seen Spokey Withers for so long that he suspected Dunc Mickle of making a check on his own movements.

"I suppose Jack can be watching me, the same as I watch him," he told himself. "Lord knows, we both get plenty of chance."

One of his reasons for riding to the Cross 8 had been for the purpose of persuading Deane that he was not being watched. It had been driven in on him that Deane had acted with a certain shrewdness in pretending to remain in the employ of the Cattlemen's Association. With this excuse, Jack was able to confer with Mickle at will. Although Robuck knew about every meeting which had taken place between the two for a week, he knew nothing of what had passed. Jack's promise to keep him posted on any lead the Association turned up, was the most transparent of blinds.

Reaching Wade Shandler's office, Robuck turned in there. Shandler cocked an inscrutable, rooster-like eye at him under the brim of his hat.

"Givin' yore hoss some exercise?" he grunted.

"Yes," said Robuck seriously. "Wade, what do you know about Devlin's activities for the past week?"

"Nothin'," said Shandler succinctly. Robuck queried him at length, but the sheriff knew no more than the ranchers and cowboys concerning the outlaws' disappearance. It appeared an indisputable fact, and that was all.

"Be all right with me if he's never heard of again," said Shandler, with unction.

"But you don't expect anything like that."

"No," gloomily. "Dunno's I do."

Repairing to the Ox-Yoke, later, Robuck found Jack Deane sitting in at a card game. He looked up genially, nodded, and went on playing. It seemed to Robuck that since he had been shot, he spent a large share of his salary, if not all, on amusements. This time, however, he seemed to be winning. The game went on all afternoon, and Robuck looked in only once or twice to make sure Jack was still there. It gave him a liberty of movement he had not had in town for some time; but it appeared he would gain nothing from it.

Deane left the game at supper-time for a hasty meal, then returned. The men at the table with him changed from time to time, but he stayed on. A second mound of chips began to grow at his elbow. In the absence of better game, Robuck took to watching Dunc Mickle.

The banker ate his supper late, enjoyed a cigar while talking with various men on the street, and then returned to the bank. Robuck took up his stand across the way, watching with timeless patience. It was ten o'clock, and he had just returned from his latest trip to make sure of Deane's whereabouts, when he almost missed the shadow which flitted past the bank and disappeared in the alley siding it.

Instantly alert, he crossed the street, following the darker shadows, and stole toward the alley. It might well be the trail of an unrelated intrigue which he had crossed, he knew; but he did not think so. A moment later, moving down the alley with utmost caution, he was sure of his ground. He had been in time to catch the disappearing flash of light as the rear door in the bank building was closed. Reaching it in an instant, he hearkened, tense, to the receding murmur of voices within. Dunc Mickle had let someone in the back way. The question was—who?

Trying the door softly and finding it locked, Robuck returned to the front of the bank. The shade in the front window had been pulled up so that a band of light no more than a foot wide showed at the top. The door afforded no glimpse within—yet he had to know who it was who had joined Mickle in the bank.

He rejected the expedient of waiting until the man should emerge, and was considering bringing a bronc so that he could stand in the saddle and see in at the top of the big window, when a better idea occurred to him.

Across the street stood a sagging wagon shed. Its beams shuddered when he tried them, but they held. A moment later, crawling over the shaky roof, he reached the outer edge—and found himself gazing across the street, through the unshaded strip of window in the bank, at Dunc Mickle and the man who talked with him. And that man was Spokey Withers.

"Huh!" Robuck grunted involuntarily. And then, silently to himself: "I don't know why that should surprise me, either. It's exactly what I expected, sooner or later."

But, clambering back to the ground, he was caught up by a tension which would not release him. After all his speculation and his suspicions, at last he had something tangible to go on. There could no longer be any doubt that Spokey's devious trail spun the invisible web extending between Smoke Devlin, Dunc Mickle,

Jack Deane, and all the other ramifications of the gang preying on the range. What Dale Barron had had to say about Dunc Mickle's financial situation, plus the knowledge that Dunc had but recently bought up all the ranches he controlled; had wanted to buy the Cross 8 and had bid on other spreads, marked his place in the plot. It was all plain reading.

But knowledge was not proof. For a moment Robuck felt the heavy downpress of unsurmountable circumstance—the feeling of battling against impregnable forces, which, perhaps, had persuaded Jack Deane to throw in with the men in power.

But it was not his way to give up. His mind busy with the task which faced him, he hurried to the stable and got up his pony. Taking the back street in star-shot darkness, he drew in and dismounted in a yard a few doors from the bank. Then he returned to the alley by which Spokey had entered the building.

It was near midnight when Spokey came out. He stole to the street, Robuck following at a safe remove; and reaching his bronc at the public corral, swung up and jogged out of town. Robuck got his own mount in a hurry and set out to trail him, if possible.

It was almost dawn when the latter returned to Flathead. He had traced Spokey for miles across the range, only to lose him at last, despite his best efforts. Disgusted with himself, he stabled his bronc and repaired to his room in the hotel. Much as he wished to pursue the thread of thought this night's experiences evoked, he was asleep almost at the minute his head touched the pillow.

He awoke suddenly and opened one eye. It was broad daylight. He must have slept for several hours. Someone was at the door—someone who couldn't wait; for whoever it was, was coming in. Robuck's eye drooped shut, and there was no indication of alertness in him as he lay. He heard the gentle squeak of the door-hinge, but no step. Stealing a peek through barely parted lashes, he was startled to find Jack Deane gazing intently down at him.

Robuck would not have betrayed his wakefulness then for anything. He was curious to know what the other would do. Deane, believing him still asleep, turned to the bureau. Robuck's holstered gun lay there, under his hat. For a moment Deane fumbled with it. He made no noise, and as his back was turned, it was impossible to see what he was doing. Afterward, he turned for another searching look at Robuck. The latter lay unmoving, breathing regularly. Deane turned toward the door and stole out. The door closed with extreme gentleness, but Robuck heard the light click as the key turned in the lock, from the outside.

Sitting up abruptly, as he listened to feet retreating down the stairs, Robuck frowned. "What in hell can his game be?" he wondered.

He wasted no time in speculation, jumping out and hastily pulling on his clothes. When he came to his gun, instead of buckling it on, he removed the shells and shook one of them close to his ear. The faint tinkle of a few loose grains of powder rattling against the brass, came to him—nothing more. He grunted.

"Drew the powder out of 'em," he murmured, and

replaced the doctored cartridges with good ones. "What am I supposed to be stacking up against now?"

Had nothing else been done, he would have looked for a gun-fight later in the day; but Deane's locking the door of his room was a warning that the time element was involved. He examined the door, found he could not get through it without too much noise, and turned to the window.

It looked out across a narrow alley, over the roof of a black-smith shop next door, and with typical cow-country indifference to fresh air, had been nailed shut. However, that was soon remedied. Opening the sash, he climbed into the window-frame, poised there, and with a light leap, dropped on the roof of the blacksmith shop. It slanted slightly to the rear, toward a cluttered yard. Robuck jumped to a wagon-bed and thence to the ground, swung over the fence, and, via the alley, emerged on the street.

The sun beat down from almost directly overhead. The drowsing quiet indicated the hour of noon. Robuck stood undecided, asking himself what to expect, when his glance fell on a body of mounted men, just drawing up before the bank. Moving deliberately, they swung down and started to enter the building, three of them in the lead.

Despite the downglare of the sun, a shiver of coolness ran over Robuck's skin. This was a familiar scene to him. Warning streaked along his nerves. He knew that except for an odd customer, only Mickle and one cashier were in the bank. The circumstance was ideal for a hold-up—and that, something told him in a flash, was what this was.

Instead of starting down there, he whirled and headed at a run for the sheriff's office. If Shandler was down the street in a hash-house— He wasn't. He sat in his old swivel chair with a glum evpression on his face. His feet came down off his desk with a thump as Robuck burst in.

" A bunch of men just rode up together and stepped in the bank. I think it's a stick-up," Robuck told him swiftly.

Shandler didn't wait to ask questions. A craggy look leaping to his lean, mustached visage, he snatched up a rifle and headed for the door.

"Mike Bingle's in the blacksmith shop," he threw out. "Get him, and anybody in there with him! I'll grab some others!"

Robuck flung across the street. Bingle, a big, swarthy-faced individual, paused with hammer upraised to stare at him.

"Hold-up!" Robuck threw at him. "Drop that and grab a gun!"

Big Mike let out a bellow, his hammer clattering. Gun in hand, he started without waiting to jerk off his leather apron. "Where is it?" he ripped out.

"Down at the bank!"

They dashed out of the shop on a run. Three other men came hurrying with Shandler, armed with rifles and shotguns. Wade delayed to yell into the doorway of a store. Its proprietor gaped with astonishment at what he heard. But a moment later he scuttled out.

Only the ponies at the rail stood before the bank as Robuck charged down there. Even as he drew near, Big Mike panting at his shoulder, a man burst out of the bank with six-gun up-raised. It was Roy Olds. Seeing them, he crouched with a snarl. Smoke bloomed as he flung hasty shots at them, whirled, and ran to the ponies, yelling a warning.

The outlaws poured out of the bank. There were seven of them. Gunfire crashed as they faced the approaching men. The latter returned the fire with interest, Wade Shandler bawling to them to close up. Suddenly, one of the outlaws staggered and fell to a knee, but went on shooting. A companion yanked him to his feet; helped him to a bronc.

Smoke Devlin, plainly recognizable, tossed a gunnysack across his saddle and started to mount, calling harsh orders. He had trouble, and so did the others; for with the lead droning a death song in the street, the broncs were milling and rearing.

The outlaw was a dauntless warrior in that swirling confusion. His nerve iron, his face flashing, oblivious to the slugs whining about him and even tugging at his clothes, he fired with a cool deadliness, jammed into submission the broncs whose terror threatened escape, and seemed to wrest success from under the very nose of failure.

That much Robuck saw. Then, jerking loose a spooky bronc at a rack near at hand, he flung aboard and headed down an alley.

"Where you goin'?" Shandler blazed at him.

Robuck didn't pause to explain, but his object was

clear in his mind. With the guns of the opposition crashing at them from only one side, it was inevitable that the outlaws, swinging away at a slashing gallop, should turn in the other direction. Once started, there would be nothing to stop them.

Flashing along the backs of half-a-dozen buildings, as he passed the bank, Robuck asked himself what he could do alone, even though he were in time to cut off the outlaws. Yet he had to do something.

His first glimpse of Smoke Devlin had warned him that something was wrong. Had he been mistaken throughout in his figuring? Or had Devlin and Mickle fallen out? If that was the case, this might be Devlin's revenge—unless there was an answer behind all this which he didn't see yet. He didn't know. But one thing was sure: This was his chance to break the case wide open. And only the capture of Devlin would insure success. Could he manage it?

The pound of guns informed him that the fight still raged. It had continued for perhaps less than two minutes; but it seemed like twenty. Bursting into a cross-street, he swung the corner at a mad speed. Then he was yanking in his bronc with an iron hand. Scarcely had it slid to a halt in a cloud of dust, when he leaped to the ground and dashed toward the head of a double-team standing at the corner of the intersection.

Grabbing the head-stalls, he yanked the team into motion. The stolid draught-horses refused to move quickly, and Robuck, dragging at them with all his strength, muffled a curse in his throat. Would he be in time? Could he possibly make it? The crackle of firing still sounded around the corner; but with it came the staccato clatter of racing hoofs.

His object was to stall the team across the street so as to cut off escape for the outlaws. He was past the corner now. Flinging a look, he saw them sweeping down on him, Devlin in the lead. He threw up his gun and snapped a warning shot. The team he was leading tossed their heads, stamping to a halt; but with a lurch, he got them started again. They were almost across now, the big wagon lumbering into position, blocking almost the full width of the street.

Devlin charged down upon Robuck, his gun flaming. Slugs fluttered past Robuck's head; one knocked off his hat. As the outlaw's horse loomed close, he flung a shot which took Devlin in the waist, and threw himself down. Something within him congealed at thought of those slashing hoofs; he rolled over madly. At the last moment, however, Devlin's bronc swerved. Smoke lifted it over a menacing hitching-post. In an instant, the outlaw was in the clear and pounding down the street toward the open.

His partners were not so lucky. Devlin's escape was cut off for them, as Robuck sprang up to complete his maneuver. Their broncs piled up against the freight wagon like trapped mustangs; they whirled to face the down-charging body of men closing up the rear, the guns of half of them empty.

"Stick 'em up, Olds!" Robuck flashed, leaping toward the outlaw, his gun threatening.

Roy Olds was game. He threw his empty gun, missed, and dived at Robuck from the saddle. Robuck sprang aside. His gun-barrel cracked Olds alongside the head. The outlaw tumbled in the dust, rolled over and relaxed.

Meanwhile Shandler and his men had not been idle. With the exchange of a few more shots, the remainder of the outlaws were quickly cornered, yanked out of the saddle, and put in custody.

Shandler was snapping on the manacles, and scores of men were pouring into the street, dazed and excited with the suddenness of the thing, when they heard a shout from down the street. Everyone looked that way. Dunc Mickle came running, waving his arms.

"Thirty thousand dollars!" he screeched. "They cleaned it out! The bank's ruined!" He broke off, looking startled, when he saw the prisoners. "Did you get 'em all?" he blurted impellingly.

Shandler stared at him and shook his head shortly. "Devlin got away with the money," he growled.

Robuck watched a peculiar expression rush into the banker's face. He did not have to wonder what it meant. Mickle hadn't wanted Smoke Devlin to be captured!

"Snag a bronc, Shandler!" he barked. "I got Devlin dead center, when he jumped me; he's in a bad way. I think we can overhaul him!"

Shandler, hearing, yelled orders for others to take charge of the prisoners. A moment later he, Robuck, and several other men got away to a flying start, stringing out as they took up the trail of the fleeing outlaw.

XIX: *With His Boots* On

DEVLIN'S trail was not hard to follow. He had begun to bleed almost immediately; dark splotches marked the dust.

"He's hard hit!" Shandler called ahead to Robuck. "He won't git far 'fore he flops outa the hull!"

Robuck would have been of the same opinion had he not known the immense stamina of the outlaw. Devlin was made of whale-bone and steel. Even so, it seemed impossible that he could hold out long. Yet as the trail ran on and on, and the racing posse caught no glimpse of the fugitive, it began to look as if this would develop into a grim chase.

Devlin had taken the plain trail winding south and west toward the Blackfoot desert. There was not the slightest difficulty in sticking to it. But roving that trail ahead in imagination, Robuck saw method in the man's madness. After some miles the trail branched—and one branch ran south to lose itself in the *malpais*.

Shandler's thoughts had taken him this far as well. Turning in the saddle, he waved urgently for those behind to forge up.

"If Devlin gits into the lava beds, we'll lose him!" he yelled.

Nor was his fear without grounds. Whatever the outlaw's method, he was beginning to get results. Farther and farther apart lay the blood-smears marking the trail. The undeviating tracks of Devlin's bronc were in no respects like the telltale, wavering advance of a dangerously wounded rider.

Something like savage despair swept Robuck as these facts became clear to him. For a time, in the face of Devlin's daring robbery, he had feared that all his calculations were thrown out. It had given him a feeling of futile emptiness difficult to over-ride. Dunc Mickle's raucous and immediate claim that the bank was ruined, however, had made him see a great light. He felt certain that more than anyone else suspected would develop out of the capture of Smoke Devlin. And now Devlin had better than a fifty-fifty chance of getting away.

With his gang captured and broken up, moreover, Smoke was unlikely to stand upon the order of his going. He would ride on out of this country. Once he was gone, the riddle of his relations with Dunc Mickle might never be finally solved.

Forty minutes passed, to the drum of racing hoofs. Not once, in this rolling land where the trail pitched up and down continuously, did they sight the fleeing quarry; but from the high ridges they began to see the flash of the dazzling lava beds, a few miles ahead.

Coming to the fork in the trail, they found that Devlin had indeed swung unerringly to the south, toward the up-tossed, flint-hard haven where not even the faint scratches of flying horse-shoes could be traced far. Here, for the first time, was the unmistakable evidence of weakening in the man they pursued. As his pony took the swing in the trail, Devlin had swayed perilously. They saw where the bronc wavered momentarily before lining out in the new direction.

"By Gawd, we'll drive him to a stand-still!" Shandler burst out harshly, seeing this. "He can't be more'n a mile or two in the lead!"

Without remitting his efforts, Robuck found it impossible to echo the sheriff's hard faith in the results of the chase. Whether it was premonition, or simply doubt, he feared they had delayed too long in getting away; that just when he was so desperately needed, Devlin would succeed in giving them the slip.

When, ten minutes later, they pounded up to the edge of the outspread *malpais,* he was sure of it. Devlin's trail ran straight into a lava gully and faded out. A lump like lead rose in Robuck's chest to suffocate him with chagrin.

He refused to show it. "We've got to work fast now!" he cried to Shandler. "This stuff will jar him to pieces in half-a-mile!"

They swept into the lava beds with but slight diminution of their speed. The disappearance of Devlin's tracks troubled them none at all.

"Spread out!" Shandler called. "We'll sweep a big scope of this stuff, quick as God'll let us!"

The posse swung into the radiating gullies and hollows and pushed on. And now they rode with guns out; for with the outlaw's trail a thing of the past, all they could hope for was to close up on the man himself.

Robuck took a middle course, Shandler paralleling

him. The glare of the lava was intense and burning under the sun; its knifelike edges menaced them on every hand. A fall of the pony here—even the slightest uncertainty—would mean broken bones and frightful gashes.

Screwing his eyes up, Robuck thrust on until he felt certain they had lost the scent altogether. Devlin had slipped away in this hostile maze, where the smallest hidden depression would be sufficient to conceal him and his horse. He had eluded them this easily! Robuck was resigning himself to the bitter knowledge, when suddenly he threw himself aside—yanked his bronc down to a chopping, sliding halt—and throwing his gun up, stared.

Devlin's horse stood with hanging head and heaving sides a dozen yards away. Devlin himself lay on the crumbling lava, bleeding once more, but conscious, and trying to force himself over on his back.

Taking this in in a flash, Robuck flung out of the saddle. He slipped dangerously on the lava, caught himself, and with a long stride, kicked the gun out of Devlin's fingers just as the muzzle brought to bear on him. A flicker of violence faded from Smoke's deep black eyes as he fell back. Robuck knelt quickly, caught him by the shoulders, and dragged him to a level spot. Then rising, he threw three ringing shots into the air, spaced.

"Wal, I'm damned!" were Shandler's first words, as he drew in near at hand. "Yuh was right, Robuck. This rough goin' cut him plumb to pieces—somethin' even he didn't figure on!"

He walked over and examined the outlaw. Robuck met the rest of the posse as it came up.

"Devlin's in bad shape," he told them. "We've got to get him out of here and to a doctor."

"Hold on, Robuck," Shandler cut in on him. "It's too late for that stuff, and Devlin knows it. He wants to talk to yuh."

Turning, Robuck moved to Smoke's side. He noted his pallor and his parched look, and straightened. "Anybody's saddle have a canteen on it?" he queried anxiously, knowing how much a few drops of water would mean to the wounded man.

No water was available, but one man produced a pint flask of whisky. "Mebby this'll do," he grunted. "I hear Devlin drinks it like water when he can get it!"

Taking it without comment, Robuck knelt and applied the bottle to Smoke's lips. The outlaw took a long pull and sighed. "Thanks, Robuck," he managed. "I was—needin' somethin' like—that. Yo're the gent that put me where I am, but I—don't hold it against you. Reckon it was—you or me!"

"What did you want to say to me?" Robuck asked. "You may not have long to talk," he added, noting the spreading gray in the man's face, and realizing that the sheriff was right. Devlin never would get beyond the lava beds again in life.

"Wal, I got plenty to—spill," Smoke whispered. "Reckon I kin—begin anywheres."

With Wade Shandler helping to support him, Devlin told a story of plotting and double-dealing which, during the last few days at least, Robuck could have foreshadowed. It was no surprise to him; but the sheriff's mouth popped open while Smoke gasped on.

He told how Dunc Mickle had protected him and given him information regularly, so that he not only evaded the Association detectives, the Wells-Fargo men and the sheriff's office successfully, but knew when and where to strike when he planned his raids.

"Where we—made our mistake was—in stickin' too long," Devlin grinned weakly.

"Whyn't yuh pull out long ago?" Shandler demanded.

"Why should we? We were—well off. Had a good thing. Protection in—town. I thought it—was cast iron." Smoke added that periodically he had allowed a couple of his boys to ride out of the country, sometimes as far as Cheyenne, to spend their money and take it easy for a spell.

"Where does Dunc Mickle fit into this?" Shandler demanded suspiciously. "He was well off. Never went outside the law 't I know of. Why'd he need yuh?"

Devlin panted out an explanation which Robuck had already largely pieced together. Tortured by dreams of power, and impatient of his slow progress by normal business methods, Mickle had conceived the plan of having the ranches he coveted rustled until near-ruin brought them to his hands. Shandler's swarthy face grew dark as he listened; for Smoke's story was indeed borne out by the facts. All of the three ranches the banker now controlled had come to him through forced sale.

"Wal, then what the hell's his game, havin' yuh jack

up the bank?" Wade growled. "That was the way of it, wasn't it?"

Smoke nodded weakly. "I was goin' to—split with him," he whispered.

Shandler's visage hardened. "Thirty thousand dollars, outa his own bank! The danged skunk!"

Devlin almost laughed. "Get the—sack off my—saddle," he croaked. "It's all—there. All I got."

Robuck sprang up to comply. A moment later he came back, turning the gunny-sack inside out. A small bundle of currency was all he found.

"There's only a thousand or so here," he said. "It could have been shoved in a man's pocket!"

Devlin did laugh. "The bag was—fer looks," he got out. "The way Mickle—wanted it to look. He overplayed his hand. The bank was short—he expected an examiner in a week or two—he had to do—somethin'."

"So he covered his swindle this way—and offered yuh half of a thousand dollars fer throwin' away yore life!" Shandler exploded. "Devlin, yo're a damn fool!"

"There was—more to it—than that," Smoke hastened to explain. "It was—part of our plans. He swore we'd be safe. All the—steers we rustled was—clear profit."

"Devlin," Robuck put in quickly; "there's a few things I want to ask you, just for the record. Did you, or any of your men, ever take a shot at me? Did one of you kill Red Lefler?"

"No!" Smoke got out strongly. "Yuh know we didn't, Robuck! That ain't our style!"

Robuck nodded. He had not been wrong about Lafe Rash.

"And Jack Deane?" he persisted.

Something came into Devlin's eyes then, a shadow of stubbornness. "Reckon I'd have got him—if I'd had the—chance," he muttered. "He wasn't like—you."

"What yuh mean?" Shandler queried instantly. "What about Deane?"

Smoke did not answer; but his reply to Robuck's next question was an answer to Shandler as well.

"Devlin," said Robuck slowly, "why are you telling me all this?" It had struck him throughout that the outlaw bore Dunc Mickle a grudge, the vehemence of which had given him strength to tell his story.

Smoke's eyes sharpened. "He didn't play—square," he husked. "Mickle promised me he'd—keep yuh outa that hold-up, Robuck. Deane was to—take care of it. He bungled! Or else Dunc decided this'd be a fine way of gettin' rid of me! I'm—squarin' accounts before it's too—late."

He stiffened as his last words trailed off, and his eyes glazed.

"He's goin'!" Shandler exclaimed. "My Gawd—what a yarn he had to tell!" He watched the light die out of the outlaw's face, like a candle extinguished behind a window, then drew a long breath. "Reckon this explains a lot to me, Robuck," he grunted, getting to his feet. "A thousand dollars! Why—that must be all the bank had!" It touched him personally, for he had had three or four times that amount on deposit in the bank himself—the savings of years.

"Mickle's got something to answer for," Robuck nodded. "I knew what he was up to several days ago, but how I was going to put the deadwood on him was another matter. He seems to have accommodated by doing it himself."

Shandler stared. "Yuh mean to say yuh knew all this—about Mickle and Deane and all?" he queried.

"Yes." But Robuck was frowning. "I wish I'd thought to ask Devlin who it was who killed Daggett. He was square, and he died for it. Perhaps if we can pick up Spokey Withers, he'll tell. Maybe it was Spokey himself."

Shandler knew from Devlin's story that Spokey had been the go-between for him and Mickle. He nodded to Robuck's last suggestion.

"It was likely him, all right. Spokey was mixed up in a rustlin' muss ten years or more ago. All the others was killed, in the end; Spokey told a story about 'em fightin' together over money, and there wasn't nobody to contradict him. I see that business in a new light, now. Spokey got a couple years in Deer Lodge, and that was the end of it."

"Maybe we can nail Withers in Flathead, if he hasn't taken warning and drifted."

"Deane too," Shandler concurred grimly.

It was decided to pack Smoke Devlin out of the *malpais* to town. Leaving a couple of men to take care of this, Robuck and the sheriff went on ahead. They felt certain that with all he had at stake, Dunc Mickle would remain where he could be found until he knew definitely that all was lost.

"Remember that Horan business," Robuck told Shandler, as they rode. "You can't walk up to Mickle and accuse him of what we know, slap him in jail and expect to hold him. This ranching community will bust wide open when it learns."

Wade assented. "I shore don't wanta go through that business again, by golly! Let's see . . ." He thought a moment. "Tell yuh what. We'll swear out a warrant, then wait. We won't git back to town more'n an hour before seventeen comes through. A little before, I'll serve Mickle, we'll walk to the train and git on without no fuss. Yuh can spill the news after she pulls out."

"How about Spokey and Deane?" Robuck queried. "Neither one of them will give up without trouble. If they see Mickle leaving, it may be the tip-off to them, and they'll skip."

"We'll jest have to take our chances with 'em," Shandler replied. "Dunc's the big fish I'm anglin' for. I won't take no chances with him at all."

Since Mickle was the crux of the case he had worked so long to solve, Robuck could not demur; but he felt a resentment against Jack Deane which made him uncertain of how he would act when he met the other face to face.

Arriving in town, they found it in a state of tense excitement. The members of Devlin's gang had been lodged in jail and their various wounds cared for. The news of the hold-up had spread over the range with surprising celerity. Already ranchers were beginning to drift in. Their mood became ugly when they learned that the bank had been cleaned out. Many depended on the financial institution for their welfare.

Robuck got a glimpse of Dale Barron and his daughter, but he remained away from them. There was too much else to attend to for the present. He and Shandler rode down to the bank, picking up a group of followers as they went.

Dunc Mickle was at the bank, talking excitedly to the ranchers who had come to consult him. A furtive look flashed across his face when he saw that Robuck and Shandler had already returned. It was gone as quickly as it had come, and Mickle thrust forward to front them boldly.

"Well, did he get away from you?" he demanded.

Shandler eyed him inscrutably. "He did, if yuh call dyin' gettin' away, Dunc," he said. "Devlin is dead. The boys're bringin' him in now."

Mickle weathered an inward storm, his face changing. But he grasped at straws.

"Dead when you found him, eh?" he barked.

The sheriff let silence answer for him; and Dunc grasped at the interpretation he most desired. "Did you get the money he took from the bank?" he flung out keenly.

"We found 'bout a thousand dollars on him," Shandler told him.

The men in the bank gathered around, muttering, at this intelligence. Mickle himself went blank. He seemed groping. Suddenly he found himself.

"He must have hidden the rest of it!" he got out

loudly. "Didn't you look around, where you found him?"

Robuck had a swift picture of where he had found Devlin, obviously flung out of his saddle, and broken where he lay. But he said nothing.

"Wal, we didn't find nothin'," Shandler answered dryly. "I'll go and talk to Devlin's men now." He turned away from the crafty expression of relief in Mickle's eyes, afraid that his own look of loathing and disgust would give him away before he was ready.

He and Robuck turned out of the bank, after answering questions put by the aroused ranchers. But they did not proceed immediately to the jail. Shandler first swore out a warrant for Dunc Mickle's arrest, charging grand-larceny and conspiracy, intent to defraud and the aiding and abetting of criminals. Then, while Shandler headed for the jail, Robuck paused long enough to murmur a few words, and started away on his own errand.

First he repaired to the hotel, then to the Ox-Yoke. The saloon was jammed with men, discussing the day's events. The murmur died down at Robuck's entrance. Every man looked to him in obvious respect, for one and all understood the difficulties and obstacles against which he had been struggling, or thought they did. The story of his trapping Smoke Devlin's gang with the aid of a freight team was already in the process of becoming a range classic. He found it impossible to buy a drink. But, leaving the place a few minutes later, he knew that Jack Deane had not been seen since the hold-up.

"I'm afraid he knows where he stands, and has pulled his freight," he mused, shaking his head. But he did not let it go at that, making a quick survey of the town on the off chance of picking up Spokey Withers. Spokey, however, had apparently crawled his bronc in the same fashion as Deane had done.

Robuck gave up and walked down to the jail. As he stepped in, Shandler stood in the office, glancing at his battered watch. He looked up and nodded.

"Waitin' fer you," he said. "It's four now. We'll go up to the bank. We got to get Mickle alone to serve the warrant on him; and if them ranchers are still there, I'll leave it to you to stall 'em off long enough fer me to git Dunc to the train."

"Okay."

They swung out of the jail and down the street. Mickle and his tellers were busy in the bank, but fortunately the other men had left.

Shandler called Mickle aside. The banker's keen glance flamed with instant suspicion. He raked Robuck's inscrutable face and turned warily on Shandler.

"What is it?" he snapped. "Did you find anything out, down at the jail?"

"What I know, Mickle, I found out before I went down there," Wade told him levelly. "I've got a warrant here fer yore arrest." He produced it. "Will you come quietly, or— Hold it!" he ripped out, as Dunc made an abortive gesture toward his back pocket. "Lift yore arms, Mickle, while Robuck gets yore gun . . . That's better. Now, if you wanta read this—"

But Mickle understood only too well what he was charged with. "Devlin wasn't dead when you found him!" he charged. "He talked—he lied! I can tell you almost the exact story he gave, and not a word of it is true—"

"I daresay you can tell me, all right," Shandler rejoined curtly. "We'll let a court decide whether it's true or not. Get yore hat, Dunc. We got about five minutes to catch seventeen; and yo're takin' it with me."

Mickle swung on Robuck furiously. "You're responsible for this!" he snarled. "Damn you, I wish I'd had you cut down long ago!"

"Mickle, get yore hat!" Shandler shot at him sharply.

He followed close while Dunc moved to pick up his hat from the top of his desk. Not a move he made escaped the sheriff's keen watchfulness.

"Now," said the latter easily. "We'll walk down to the station and climb aboard. If anybody speaks to you, Mickle, tell 'em it can wait till later. I'm warnin' yuh—if yuh don't git out of Flathead quietly, and damn soon, you'll never get out!"

Mickle blanched as the import of the warning sank home. With Shandler and Robuck at his heels, he strode out of the bank without a backward look, and headed for the railroad station.

Seventeen shrieked as they walked out on the platform. A few minutes later, Dunc and Shandler climbed aboard the passenger coach. A number of people watched their departure without suspecting its significance. Robuck waited till the train pulled out, and then turned as Cal McDonough, pale and stiff from his recent wound, approached.

"Where's Mickle and Shandler goin', Robuck?" the latter asked. "They got a lead some'eres up the line on more of the bank money?"

Robuck shook his head. "Mickle's heading for Two-spot and trial, McDonough," he said. "He was behind all these rustling raids you've suffered. He was protecting Smoke Devlin. He got Devlin to stick up the bank to cover his own shortages. It'll mean twenty years or more for him." In a few words he rounded out the rest of the story.

McDonough stared. "What!" he gasped. "Yo're tellin' me Mickle is a rat—that he was robbin' us, puttin' all this hell on us—and you nailed him at it?"

"It sums up to that," Robuck admitted. "Kind of makes a clean sweep of things, doesn't it?"

XX: *The Home Trail*

SO FAST did the story of Dunc Mickle's villainy travel that a few minutes sufficed to carry it the length and breadth of Flathead. Robuck saw knots of men in the street, discussing the affair with heated, dangerous calmness. This town could almost be heard to boil.

Himself, Robuck was curiously dispassionate. For the first time, the driving necessity which had held him in the Flathead country was relaxed. Although he could expect no reward for his work, there was satisfaction in him too: a satisfaction marred by the knowledge that unfinished business remained, which would carry him away from this range on a long trail.

"My boy, you've no right to wear that expression this afternoon," a voice from the hotel porch startled him. He looked up. In Dale Barron's eyes was a faintly questioning light; but Virginia's look was wholly approving. Robuck's faint scowl vanished as he joined them.

"You've done work today," Dale proceeded, "that no man need be ashamed of. It wipes out that train robbery that got yore dander up, in fine style. But more'n that, Robuck, it gives us ranchers a breathin' spell. It gives us a chance to see daylight ahead once more. We can stop worryin' about our stock bein' rustled, and havin' our ranches stole out from under us. We got you to thank for it all, and I reckon you know how we feel."

Robuck met his steady gaze with veiled admiration on his own part. Dale Barron had lost his son, and nearly lost his ranch; and responsible for it had been a man whom he had trusted. Yet instead of being dazed and resenting, he was sober and hopeful and calm, in sharp contrast to the men who grumbled wrathfully because Dunc Mickle had been put beyond their reach.

"I only did what I saw before me to be done," said Robuck quietly. He met Virginia's eye and smiled faintly.

"I know. But Jack Deane, now—" Dale began, only to break off abruptly at sight of the look which flashed into Robuck's face. "Whatsa matter?" the rancher queried keenly.

"Nothing," Robuck replied, with an effort.

"Deane must've stepped on yore toes proper," Dale insisted shrewdly. "Where is he? . . . You ain't tellin' me he was mixed up in this business, too?" he demanded suspiciously.

There was nothing to be gained by evasion. Other men already knew. Robuck admitted that such was the case; and that, seeing himself discovered, Deane had evidently taken refuge in flight.

"Aw—!" exclaimed Barron gruffly. "That's hard lines."

But it was Virginia who read in Robuck's flat lipped, expressionless face how hard it was for him. "Let's not talk about it any more," she abruptly cut off her father's further inquiries.

"Wal—that's right," Dale conceded. "Reckon I better git goin', anyway. Looks like Cal McDonough was callin' a meetin' of the Association, right now. Yuh be around," he told Robuck, "and mebby I'll have somethin' to say to yuh later."

He got up and walked off the porch, at McDonough's beckoning wave. Robuck and Virginia were left to themselves.

"Father is not the same man he was, a week, or even a few hours, ago," she said gently. "You will receive many thanks for what you have done, Bill; none more sincere than mine, for giving back to me the father I used to know. He has dropped ten years off his shoulders."

Robuck stirred uncomfortably.

"I know how gratitude affects you at this time," she went on softly. "It makes you remember that you have lost Red, and that another you called a friend has betrayed you."

"It's not that alone," Robuck broke in, almost harshly. "It's knowing how far Jack would go. I could stand his changing sides, but—" He broke off.

She waited understandingly.

"Virginia, I recognized the writing in that note that took you to Granite Basin," he told her bluntly.

"I guessed that you did . . . It was Jack's?"

He nodded briefly, his face hard.

"I figured out, at the time, that he expected you to

take the old coulee trail, and intended to stop you on the way."

"But why, if he went to all that trouble getting me to go?" Virginia wanted to know.

"He didn't want you there. He wanted me to think you had gone there, and follow you—as I did."

"And if I hadn't been there, when you came—?" She caught at the possibilities. Her face paled.

"Devlin would have had other ideas about what to do with me," he said simply. "But I would have met that, in my own way. It's you I'm thinking about. Jack let you start for that place—and then got himself shot—"

"By that Rash, the Wyoming rustler? Father told me," she interposed. Sensing that it eased him to talk, she quietly led him on.

But they got no further then. About to proceed, Robuck paused as harsh cries from down the street drew his attention to a crowd gathering before the livery stable. He sprang up as shots sounded down there.

"What can it be?" the girl exclaimed breathlessly. She hastened down the steps at his side for a better look.

What they saw froze them to immobility. The crowd before the stable surged back. Two men who had evidently been in the barn stepped into view, with drawn guns menacing. Robuck grunted his astonishment.

"It's Deane and Spokey Withers!" he got out tensely. "They got trapped there at the stable before they got away—somebody smoked them out. They'll be killed!"

Virginia had no need to have explained for her the ugly temper of this town, or what it might lead to in the face of Dunc Mickle's escape from their summary justice. Even as she gazed, the crowd yelled threats at the two crouching men.

Jack and Spokey must have known they could not hold back the crumbling dam of vengeance for any length of time. Suddenly a gun crashed—another. Angered men crushed irresistibly forward. The two turned and ran.

Spokey made a strategic mistake. Darting toward a hitch-rack, he swarmed up on a bronc; yanked it loose, whirled. Half-a-dozen guns thundered. Spokey loosed the screech of a mortally wounded man, and jamming in the spurs, hurled the bronc like a thunderbolt of hate straight toward the crowd. But the animal was daunted. It swerved at the last moment, hard. Spokey was flung out of the saddle, to disappear among clawing hands.

He was paying, in a way, the debt Dunc Mickle had evaded. But it was more than that, too. These men knew Spokey's part in the violent death of Daggett, the Association detective. Daggett had been speedily avenged.

For Robuck, the sight of Jack Deane, pelting this way, dodging the shots of half-a-dozen pursuing men, held a sharp significance. Whirling, he grasped Virginia's arm and would have propelled her toward the hotel porch.

"Get inside!" he jerked out.

But she resisted him, standing there at gaze. "Don't mind me!" she cried. "Watch out, Bill!"

She was telling him, with a wrench in her voice, to be on his guard. And there was need of it. Deane had fastened the look of a madman on his erstwhile partner. He came charging directly toward Robuck, a smoking gun in his hand.

He was fifty yards away now, and speedily closing up the distance. "Do something!" Virginia cried imploringly. But still Robuck stood like rock, bringing the full force of his will to bear on the other man. When Deane slowed, the tension of a cougar in his blocky body, scarcely twenty yards separated them.

For Deane, trapped as he was, the sight of Robuck in this moment was like a red rag to a bull. He forgot the meager hope of escape which had jerked his legs into a wild run. Here was the man who had beaten him out—with the girl who had been the stake. That he had lost on all counts, Deane knew; and it drove him to discard what little sanity he had retained. No longer was he conscious of the wrongs he had committed against this man who had been his friend. They had turned against him; in his twisted brain, he was the injured one.

"I'll square things with you!" he spat out stridently. Hard on the words, his gun flamed.

Three times he shot, with unbelievable rapidity. But the very heat of his hatred worked against him now. Robuck felt the wicked flutter of slugs past his face. One plucked at his shirt over the heart as he stood partly sidewise. But none had struck.

With deadly certainty he whipped up his gun and fired once. An expression of amazement swept Jack Deane's distorted features. For an instant he froze, his gun unconsciously sagging. With a belated snarl he fought to raise it once more; but he could not. It bucked and pumped a slug into the dust just as he crumpled forward over it.

Men ran up, panting—to stare, when they saw Robuck still on his feet and plainly unmarked. Kneeling, one of them turned Deane over. He had been shot through the heart, and had died even as he fell.

A large part of the crowd crushing forward, to gather here, Robuck turned and guided Virginia up on the porch. She scanned his wooden countenance solicitously, but said nothing. After that, a lump rose in Robuck's throat; he didn't want to talk. She had watched him kill a man who had once been his partner; yet she forebore to condemn. But something powerful drove between them, forcing them apart. Robuck felt it. Moreover, there was a new impulse tugging at him, and one he had answered before.

Taking his leave quietly, he walked down to the stable. He paid his bill there and was saddling up, when someone approached, to stop near his stall. He looked up, and found his eyes resting on Virginia Barron's fair and faintly wistful face. For a long moment, looking at her, he maintained silence. It was she who finally spoke.

"Well, Bill—your work is done, now," she said.

He gave his cinch another tug and looked at her again. "There's always the trail ahead," he replied. "It's all that's left for me." His voice was low, and he kept it that way, because there was something in him that wanted to shout, and must not.

"A trail without a job," she reminded him. "Will you punch cows, or go back to the Pinkertons?"

A shadow crossed his face. "I don't know. Not that last. I've had enough detecting to last me from here out."

"That's too bad," she said gravely. "Because I am sure Father intended asking you to head the Cattlemen's Association."

He frowned. "I couldn't stay on here."

She stepped closer. "Couldn't you, Bill? Are you sure of that?" she asked.

"What do you mean?" he exclaimed hoarsely.

"Couldn't you—if I asked you to?" she went on, steadily and tenderly. "Drifting was all right in the past. It brought you here. But a man must settle down sometime, mustn't he? Bill, I don't want you to—go—"

She got no farther. Robuck took a short step—the longest and most important of his life, for all that—and his arms closed about her small, sturdy shoulders. He bent his head; and as their lips met, he knew suddenly and completely that for him, roaming was done. This was his home, and destiny awaited him here, at the side of a small, bright-eyed partner whose fidelity he would never be called upon to question.